Jane E. Benson

From the Lune to the Neva Sixty Years Ago

Jane E. Benson

From the Lune to the Neva Sixty Years Ago

ISBN/EAN: 9783337399771

Printed in Europe, USA, Canada, Australia, Japan

Cover: Foto ©Andreas Hilbeck / pixelio.de

More available books at **www.hansebooks.com**

FROM THE LUNE TO THE NEVA

SIXTY YEARS AGO;

WITH

ACKWORTH AND "QUAKER" LIFE

BY THE WAY.

" The doctrine of continuity is not solely applicable to physical inquiries."—W. R. GROVE.

BY

J. B.

LONDON:

SAML. HARRIS & Co., 5, BISHOPSGATE STREET WITHOUT.

1879.

PREFACE.

The necessity for binding a second 500 copies of this little book gives the writer an opportunity of complying with numerous requests for the real names of some of the characters mentioned in it. Most of them have been correctly guessed in one or other of the kind notices of the work that have appeared in various periodicals, and perhaps the object may be best accomplished by quoting from two of them sufficient to reveal the originals. The *Lancaster Observer* gives the following :—

" FROM THE LUNE TO THE NEVA, &c.—Dwellers by the Lune and particularly those in the old castle-crowned town to which it has given its name, look upon everything belonging to it with affection and loyalty. It was, therefore, with both interest and curiosity that we took up the unpretending volume bearing the above title. But instead of a comparison between the two rivers, or a narrative of travel, as might have been expected, we found it to be a simple account of two Quaker families at the beginning of this century. With the aid of a hint from " the pump " and other sources, we found that Kilvert Street means Nicholas Street, and that the old house so graphically described is the one at Stonewell, now occupied as business premises by Mr. Baxter, but for a long time in the possession of Mr. Edmondson's family—here named Skelton—well-known members of the Society of Friends. With this clue it is not difficult to discover in the " young pickle " who was taught knitting to keep him out of mischief, the future inventor of the railway ticket system, and in his younger brother a noted and experienced educator, who finished his career at Queenwood College, in Hampshire. The companion household of Dunnings must change its name to Hodgson, and will then be recognised as that of another old Lancaster family."

The Friends' Quarterly Examiner, which emanates from Southampton, after connecting the name of Daniel Brady with that of the "honoured servant of Christ, Daniel Wheeler," who was, more than a generation ago, at St. Petersburg, "holding a position of great trust and responsibility direct from the Emperor Alexander," concludes with these words:—"Possibly to us a still deeper interest is awakened in this history from the fact that, in the mysterious interweavings of the threads of our existence here, though dying in different places, the remains of Daniel Wheeler's three sons, William, Charles, and Joshua, once young pupils on the banks of the Neva, now rest together in the quiet and picturesque burying ground at Southampton; and more remarkable still, their honoured tutor and the fair blue-eyed little maiden with her sunny curls, of whom the book tells us so pleasantly, and who became a happy bride in 1821, now lie side by side in the same sweet resting-place; whilst the neat headstones giving the dates of decease reveal that six months only were they separated here on earth."

If we add to these extracts that William Doubleday, the Ackworth reading-master, was William Singleton, who afterwards established a private boarding-school at Broomhall near Sheffield (Hallam), and whose daughter, Anne, was the Margaret of the following pages, the reader will have the desired clue to the names of any importance occurring in them.

J. B.

CONTENTS.

FROM THE LUNE TO THE NEVA.

CHAPTER I.

Introducing the Two Boys.—"Let me go too, Mother."

We were sitting on the shore, in a quiet little nook—where, is of no consequence—making ducks and drakes of all the flat pebbles within our reach, and, between the throws, discussing the best opening for a tale, so as to secure as early as possible the reader's interest and attention. Cousin Fanny, an inveterate novel-reader, declared she always began in the middle: " That was how you generally got to know fresh people. You struck in to the middle of their lives and liked or disliked them, or at any rate felt so much interest in them as to wish to know something of their antecedents. And then you turned back to the first volume to learn who they were and what they had been doing before you and they first met."

A German professor, who was the one gentleman of our party, much as he admired and wished to stand well with Fanny, could not help expressing his horror of this style of reading. Novel reading at all was to him so unsatisfying as to be almost a fatigue. He had seen at the station that morning, a porter approach a large box that was standing on the platform, and prepare to lift it on to his truck. The man settled his garments, anointed his hands in the usual way, laid hold of the cord, and brought his will and strength to bear upon the task. He raised the box, and, behold, it was empty! His powers were so much in excess of the work, that, besides being ridiculous, the effect was almost painful. His superfluous effort expended itself in lifting the box too high; he received a blow in the face and narrowly escaped a fall. This illustrated his own feeling with regard to novel reading. You sat down to the perusal of a book prepared to give it your best attention, and, behold, there was nothing worth attending to! Its weight was almost *nil* and you staggered as if you had received a blow. If, however, there were intellects capable only of this nominal exertion, and he looked mischievously across at our pretty cousin, he should certainly recommend the reader to begin at the beginning, and though he could not say the same to the author, for the initial influence of a man's life lies too far in the past for human mind to trace, he would say "let us know at least as much as we can of a hero's ancestors, that we may be the better able to understand his character."

"Hear! Hear!" cried Fanny; "now, Janet, what do you say?" Practically, I agreed with her; I am afraid I often read a tale in the same disorderly fashion, but I had a pet theory, which was to remove the temptation for such practices, and briefly replied "there is generally in any life worth notice, some circumstance, often apparently trivial, which proves the turning point in its career, and is, I think, a fair point of interest to start from. And as the novelist's aim is to give us life-like pictures, the remark applies equally to fiction."

"Sententious, as usual, my dear," said our pleasant aunt and hostess; "now I will conclude the discussion, if you please, not with an opinion but a proposition. Each of you shall write a tale in the style you recommend, and we will judge which is the most tempting and agreeable to read."

We all declared we could not do any such thing; "it was easy to find fault, but difficult to improve on the faulty performance;" "one thing to suggest and quite another to carry out the suggestion," with many other sage and novel excuses which "Auntie" said had nothing to do with the matter. We had not been finding fault with any particular performance, and as to a suggestion, it was just that "quite another thing" she wanted from us. But we shook our heads, and felt hopelessly incapable. After a while, however, though remaining hopelessly incapable of producing a novel or even a tale, I remembered a life that had often interested me, and thought I would try to give a little of its simple history, especially as I had more than once heard the subject of it say the turning point with him was a speech made in boyhood, and it would therefore illustrate my theory well.

The speech my friend alluded to was a very simple one, only "Mother let me go too," but John, as we will call him—John Skelton—used to say it was what gave the direction to his future life. If he had not been a "Friend" I dare say he would have called it the "key-note" of his life, but being a member of that Society the expression did not occur to him. He was a curly-headed boy of twelve, and was at the moment finishing a basin of soup that his mother had prepared for him on his return from school.

Literally she had prepared it, for they were in humble circumstances, and Mary Skelton's own hands ministered lovingly to the wants of her household. She was an energetic, sensible, conscientious woman, a true helpmeet

to her husband, and a wise mother to his children, tending
them and working for them with a deep love and solicitude,
which, though they did not lead her to much demonstration
of affection, were felt by her family, from babyhood to
man and womanhood, as an influence pervading the home.
They knew she was their good friend and one to be relied
on, not only in childish dilemmas, but throughout their
lives whenever help and counsel were felt to be needed.
She was fertile in resources too, and had already solved the
problem of what to do with a boy's surplus energy long
before the days of Kindergartens and School Workshops.
Her second son, Harry, was a "regular pickle," always
getting into scrapes, but always getting well out of them by
the help of his twinkling eye and the good-humoured
simplicity with which he acknowledged his fault and expressed himself ready to take the consequences. " I've had
my fun and I'll go through my punishment like a brick, as
a fellow ought," was the feeling of the culprit, though he
would, no doubt, have translated it into language more
befitting a young Quaker at the beginning of this century.
But he felt also that the fun was worth what he had to pay
for it, and he was willing to purchase enjoyment again at a
similar price.

His mother, however, did not see the matter in the same
light.   His practical jokes were often inconvenient, and she
was well aware of the disadvantage of this frequent punishment.   She often said to her faithful friend and neighbour,
Elizabeth Dunning, commonly called Betsy, " I'm not on
the right plan with Henry, some how or other ; I don't like
punishments that seem set in a spirit of revenge ; I think
they should follow a fault as if you could not help it, and as

if you had nothing to do with choosing what the child must suffer or do; it ought to be so clearly a consequence of his misdeed that he could almost decide upon it himself."

" Thou would be hard set to find a natural consequence to some of Harry's pranks that would touch him," replied Betsy, "and I don't say it from unkindness either, for I'm really fond of the lad, only I'd rather thou had him to bring up than me."

" Well, if I cannot find the right way to punish, I must try and set him to something that will prevent its being needed. He can't help his love of fun, poor child! It was born with him, and often enough he only wants something to do, *but he hits upon the wrong thing.* I'll get some worsted and teach him to knit stockings. Men folk knit in Dent, where I come from, and I don't know why boys shouldn't learn here."

" Thou'lt be a clever woman," said Betsy, as she turned to go, "if thou manages him with four needles and a ball of yarn, but we shall see. And here he comes racing down Kilvert Street as hard as he can run, I wonder what he has been up to."

" I'm glad my Willie has taken up with John instead of Harry, and yet they are all fine lads," thought she as she nodded to him in passing and caught sight of her own boy and his "chum" with arms across each other's shoulders at the top of the steep narrow street up which the Skelton's house faced.

Harry was not up to mischief this time, however, he was only meaning to rush up the yard to a three-feet square garden they had begged soil for, and had edged with bits of flag picked up in the stone quarries.

"Henry!" called his mother, as he dashed into the passage that separated the shop from the house-place or parlour; "Henry!"

"Yes, Mother; does thou want me? I'm in such a hurry, I sowed some mustard and cress this morning, and I want to see if it has come up."

"Go thy way then, but don't scratch the seed up to look, and come back to me, I want to ask thee something."

"Whatever does Mother want me for," wondered the boy, accustomed to be 'wanted' only for misdemeanours; but mother's word was law, so he merely glanced at the precious bed as yet unpierced by shoots, and was back again by her side before the other two were at the bottom of the hill.

She greeted him this time with "Harry," and the name at once reassured him. "I have been wishing thou could help me about father's stockings; he wants some new ones badly, and I think thou could learn to knit and make him a pair. Both my brothers used to knit."

"And so will I, Mother, I should like to."

"So thou shall then; I will buy some worsted this afternoon, and thou can begin to learn the stitch to-night."

The point was gained thus far. One day, some months later, he was sitting on a stool demurely handling his 'pins,' and humming to himself the Dale knitting ditty,

"Rinnin on a silver edge nine mile lang,
Gin a let a loup down back mun a gang,"

when one of the well-to-do members of their community entered the shop, and, crossing the lobby, knocked at the parlour door. After a kindly greeting to Mary, her attention was drawn to the little fellow on the "cricket" by the hearth.

"He is knitting father a pair of stockings," was the reply to her enquiring look.

"I am well pleased to see it," said the Friend. "When they are finished, Henry, thou mayst bring them to show to me."

The correct inflection of the verb seemed appropriate from the lips of the stately lady. "You" had been objected to by the earliest Friends as wanting in simplicity and honesty. "We," they said, was originally the royal assumption of plurality of powers, while "you" was the courtier's acknowledgement of the verbal fiction, and though the flattery had gradually descended in the scale of society until its primitive meaning was lost, those true iconoclasts felt they could draw "the line of safety" only "at the bottom of the whole system."

The next generation used the manner of speech without thinking much of the reason for it, and slipped into a style as ungrammatical as the condemned one, though still keeping the singular number. "Thou mayst," however, which was practically abandoned in familar conversation, did not sound too stiff from the Friend in dove-coloured silk, who was inviting Henry to pay her a visit.

In due time the visit was paid. Half pleased, half afraid, Henry took the completed work to the house on Castle Hill, and received, beside kind words and a piece of cake, a whole shilling as an encouragement in the ways of wisdom. The sensible director of affairs at home saw her opportunity :

"I will give thee another sixpence to that if thou will spend it on a hammer and nails, Harry, and we will clear out that little garret for a workshop for thee. Thou will perhaps get a joiner's bench, and be properly set up some day."

I wonder if the Scientists would think it right to call this an example of "Conservation of Energy." It was, at any rate, the "key-note" of Harry's life, which in the fulness of time left its influence on the world, but which we cannot pursue further now. Everyone was three years older when we first looked into the sitting-room than at the time of this little episode, and Henry was apprenticed to their neighbour Gilbert Dunning, who was a cabinet-maker, an arrangement which, as might be expected, suited him exactly, while John and his companion, Willie Dunning, had increased in stature and in learning, and were still, as Willie's mother had called them, three years before, "fine lads," and still fast friends.

The two mothers were companions also, sympathizing in each other's troubles and sharing each other's joys. That must be indeed a busy day on which they did not contrive to meet and compare notes or report progress. Another ball was pieced towards the "rag" carpet that was going to be woven at Whitehaven; or baby—there was always a baby at one house or the other—had cut a second tooth; homely matters that interested housewifely and motherly hearts. But not only such matters, the hearts of these two women were large and capable of taking in the difficulties and sorrows of their neighbours, not for the pleasure of talking about them, as too many of their fellow-townspeople did, but to see what they could do to help distress or mitigate suffering. The consequence was, people in need came for assistance, those in trouble came for advice, and both were sure of obtaining what they asked from these unprofessional Sisters of Charity, to the full extent of their power. In worldly goods their power was not great, but they knew how to make the best of what they had to bestow by a skilful use of needle and thread, or the wonderful alchemy of good cooking. And they were two such comfortable looking matrons, the very sight of their faces "did a body good," people said.

They had been enjoying a long chat that morning. Friargate, where the Dunnings lived, was only 'just round the corner,' and Elizabeth could easily be fetched if she were needed, so she brought her bag of mending and sat down beside her friend.

"I hope Gilbert has got the order for that sideboard he was thinking might come to him, Betsy, it would be a good thing for him, would it not?"

"Yes, he has, Mary, and more than that, he was sent for this morning to do something at the Judge's Lodgings. He is quite bright about it altogether."

But, notwithstanding the brightness, a little sigh escaped her which Mary Skelton echoed rather too feelingly. They would not have confessed it in words, even to each other, yet each knew as well as if they had spoken openly that in both houses the bread-winner was not so business-like, if that is the right word, as might be desired.

Straightforward, intelligent men they were, but lacking a something—just *the* something—which makes the difference between success and the want of it. Betsy Dunning had seen so many bright mornings end in disappointing days, that she was less sanguine than the circumstances seemed to warrant. And Mary? John Skelton senior was timid and apt to be soon discouraged, but he had bursts of daring independence that were more disastrous in their results than his periods of greatest despondency and inertia. He was one of those warm-hearted, lovable men, whom it would be least costly to their friends to maintain in idleness on condition that they kept entirely out of business. Just now he had reasonable ground for anxiety. The shipping was rapidly leaving the Lune in favour of the Mersey, and that meant the departure of his means of livelihood, for he was a ship chandler in a small way, and a sailors' general outfitter. Many of their neighbours were gone or going after the trade to Liverpool, and the question in the minds of husband and wife was, whether it was desirable to strike their tents too and follow their customers. Mary thought it would be wiser to change their business: the house and shop were in a manner their own, and she felt she could better do her share where she was known and she felt respected, than amongst strangers. She was a little influenced too by her attachment to the house, awkward and inconvenient as it was. She had walked down to it as a bride after the simple ceremony in that picturesque old "Meeting-house" on the other side of the town, and she had lived in it ever since. It was 200 years old, according to the date over the shop door, and stood on quite a large area, but as the walls were at least three feet in thickness, there was less accommodation within than its size without led you to expect. Two or three capacious cupboards were built between the outer and inner walls, and in another place there was a long, dark, narrow room that reminded one of the time when secret hiding-places were valuable, and suggested the idea that part' of the house, at least, had been built more than two centuries back. There was no uniformity in its appearance, but here a window and there a window of various shapes and sizes, just as the builder fancied when he came to each room. The one in the shop was decidedly unique; a large octagon pane of not very good glass in the centre was surrounded by square and diamond-shaped pieces of the same material arranged in their leaden frames as they could best be fitted together. Tradition had nothing to say about its origin or purpose. The children were proud to think there was not a window like it in the whole town, but their parents would have preferred more light, being honest people and not ashamed of their goods.

The passage, or lobby, as they called it, was entered from the street by a door of black oak and, like the shop and parlour, had a flagged floor. Continuing between the kitchen door on the left and the stairs foot on the right, the flagged way ran on under a skylight first, and then open to the weather, with a high wall on each side, until with an abrupt turn it finished its course in the yard before mentioned. One side of this spacious yard was occupied by a wooden shed, just now let to a weaver. His loom had not been long set up and the monotonous rhythm of his shuttle was a great attraction to the children. There were no cellars, the ground was too full of springs to permit of it.

The ends of six streets opened on the large space in front of the shop, so that it was considered rather a choice business situation, but as all the streets rose more or less from that end to the heights surrounding this centre of the old town, its sanitary position would now be considered objectionable. And yet strong men and women were reared there and lived there, with scarcely weakened powers, to a good old age. We have gained much in knowledge since the days when the "fittest" were left to "survive" as best they could, and the knowledge has mercifully tended to the diminution of suffering, but the very power of doing battle with sickness and death that it has placed in the physician's hand, has led to the survival not of the fittest only, but of a great number of the weakest as well, thereby helping to account for the degeneracy of the human race that it is so much the fashion to deplore. Mary Skelton would have found it much easier, a few months before, to support her neighbour, Nanny Jackson, whilst her leg was taken off, if the poor woman could have been under the influence of chloroform or ether, and probably the shock would have been so modified by the anæsthetic, that Nanny's system would not have succumbed and she might yet have been alive, but she could never have been the same strong woman as before her accident, and might have lingered on, a burden instead of a help to her family. The all-for-the-best was the only verdict from this point of view, hardhearted as it seems, and the optimists must seek their ground for continuing the same in the culture of the gentler, less selfish side of our characters under the new influences.

While we have been looking round and moralizing, Mary and Elizabeth have, we may be sure, been stitching and darning with the nimble fingers of workers who knew their quiet time was short.

"But that is not all I had to tell thee, Mary," her friend is saying as we return to the sitting-room; "we had a letter from Robert Whitaker this morning, and Willie can go to Ackworth the beginning of fourth month; only five weeks to get him ready in, but I think I can manage it. And his father is in such good spirits, he says he will take him to school himself. Will not that be a piece of news for Willie when he comes in?"

A wistful look came into Mary's eyes, but she only said how glad she was for them, and how ready to help in sewing or knitting if need were. *Her* boy's father was not in good spirits, and if even they had already put John's name on the list for Ackworth and there were room for him, she did not see how he could go. He must be satisfied to remain at the Friends' day school in the town; it was a very good school, and had served his brothers and his sister; it was not that, it was just a pity the two boys should be separated.

The old clock on the stairs struck twelve. It was only half-past eleven really, but that was just time to put their needles by and prepare work for knives and forks.

"Farewell, Betsy! be sure thou lets me help if thou finds thyself close pressed."

"Thank thee, Mary; thou'rt a good neighbour, farewell!"

Here was a piece of news for John, too. Poor John! and though the connection was not clear, she was glad she had such a good bowl of soup for him to-day. And he seemed to be appreciating it when we peeped at him first.

She waited till his spoon went more lazily on its journeys, and then said "The Dunnings have got their letter from Ackworth, John, and Willie is to go in about five weeks."

"Oh, mother!"

He was glad for Willie, who was anxious for the change, but heartily sorry for himself. His brothers were at business, and of his two sisters, one was old enough to have had charge of him, while the other was too young to be aught but a plaything or the spoiler of his play, as the humour seized her. He saw himself going up and down Kilvert-street alone day after day, and the vision was not a pleasant one. He and Willie had been more to each other than the real brothers on either side, and this heart-brother was going to be sent away!

" Mother, let me go too !" burst almost unconsciously from his lips.

" Thou should go if I could anyhow manage it, my dear boy, for I know what thou art feeling ; but I do not see my way to it at all."

CHAPTER II.

Dr. Fothergill.—Meetings for Discipline.—Queries.—The boys go to Ackworth.

Before proceeding further, it will be only courteous to acknowledge that both my companions of the pebbly beach had reason on their side, for not only did I in my very first chapter, in order to make my readers acquainted with our little Friend's surroundings, find myself compelled to leave him at his soup as soon as he was introduced, but I am now going to delight the heart of the Professor by looking back more than a hundred years into the past to see how it happened that so small a Society possessed an educational centre so important and excellent as the school where Willie Dunning was soon to be one of the 180 boys.

The building at Ackworth had been erected in 1757 and the following years, as a branch of the well-known Foundling Hospital in London. There was another branch at Shrewsbury, but the fate of that I do not know. Rich in subscriptions and helped by a Parliamentary grant, the governors wisely thought it would be an advantage to possess these country outlets. Their Yorkshire site they chose with great discretion. It was situated between the two villages of High and Low Ackworth, in good air and far away from smoke and dirt. They went cautiously to work too, building one year the east wing of their plan, another the centre, and next the west wing "to make the balance true."

But here ended their perfect control : the human elements required for their undertaking were less manageable·than stones and mortar. Masters and nurses were ignorant and cruel ; neglect and starvation made their usual havoc, and at the end of a sixteen years' trial, after spending £13,000 on it, the place was obliged to be closed, much to the chagrin and disappointment of its founders. It is recorded that Sir Roland Winn, "who had been an indefatigable labourer in the work," happening to visit the place at dinner-time not long after it was opened as a school, exclaimed with tears in his eyes, "why could not we have had our children as healthy and happy as these ? "

All who have visited the London Foundling Hospital of the present day, must acknowledge that the succeeding governors have discovered "why" and have acted on their experience. No one need wish to see a party of more healthy or better cared for children than those seated at the long table eating their Sunday dinner. That there is a feeling of the lack of "mothering" among them, as I have heard some mothers remark, may be only fancy, but even if a real want, the heads of the institution are not to blame for it. The children come there because, alas! there is no mother-love for them outside, or none that can avail them, and it is a love for which no institutional care can be a substitute.

Yorkshire is a long way from Middlesex ; and it was a longer way in 1757, than it is now. The world has shrunk considerably of late years. At such a distance the central committee could have little cognisance of what was going on in the lonely house upon the moor. Their hired servants felt no interest in the work and it was badly done. This was the secret of their failure.

The nearest town, about three miles away, is Pontefract, or, as it is called after the usual "clipping" process, Pomfret. In this matter of clipping, it is said that children are "the great diminutive-makers," and we may shrewdly guess they were concerned in the reduction of Pontefract. Just imagine their little mouths trying to pronounce its three syllables whenever they wanted to ask for the round black lozenges that now go by the name of Pomfret cakes! Not that I suppose the little foundlings had much experience of Pomfret cakes or even of the liquorice roots from which they are made, notwithstanding whole fields of it grew so near. Under the new régime, both were sometimes seen at Ackworth, though even then indulgence was by no means the rule as "old boys" feelingly testify.

But old boys vary. They are not all prone to looking on the dark episodes of school life, and some of them gratefully remember a kind hearted venerable master, who used to walk through their bedrooms with thumb and finger resting in his capacious waistcoat-pocket, ready to bring out a "cake" whenever he heard a cough. And they add, naïvely : "He heard a good many coughs as he came along the corridor!"

We are getting on too fast though. It was four or five years after the house was closed before the Prince of the Fairy tales appeared to put life into it again, and make its halls and corridors once more resound with children's voices.

The Prince, in this case, was a London physician, of whom it has been said, that "had not his life been 'distinguished

by a series of illustrious actions, this noble institution of
Ackworth was alone sufficient to endear his name to posterity." The posterity to whom he is endeared by his
action with regard to the school at Ackworth, is, of course,
the small portion interested in the education there, but Dr.
Fothergill's life was an influence for good to a larger circle
than could be described within the area of his co-religionists,
" Friends, commonly called Quakers."

He was a native of Wensleydale in Yorkshire, and his
modest ambition intended to be satisfied with the position of
apothecary in some country town. Fortunately for his
many patients, however, one of the professors at Edinburgh,
Dr. Munro, noted equally for his anatomical knowledge and
his power of discriminating character, induced his promising
pupil to lengthen his period of study with a view to taking
a higher standing in his profession. The result showed the
professor's discernment. To natural genius, John Fothergill
added habits of "industrious application," a combination that
never fails to lead to success.

Whether we look upon it as a special interposition of
Providence at the time, or as a consequence, no less
providential, of "all that went before," we must confess
that to a man so prepared naturally and by culture a special
sphere of usefulness is sure to be opened. He did not trouble
himself about the future; he settled as a physician in the
metropolis, and, step by step, day by day, performed the
day's duties to the best of his ability, and, to quote his own
words, "as in the sight of the God of healing."

About 1748 a fearful epidemic, somewhat akin to the
diphtheria of modern times, visited London and spread
alarm amongst all classes. Many of the wealthy and noble

3

were swept away by it, and there was general consternation. Dr. Fothergill boldly and thoroughly changed in his own practice the commonly accepted treatment of the complaint, with the most beneficial results. He became famous and rich in consequence, but this part of his success he valued only because it extended his opportunities of doing good and gave him the means of gratifying his love of nature.

His garden at Upton was known all over Europe. It was one of the "places to be seen" on the list of every intelligent foreigner visiting London. He had collected in it every plant, shrub, and tree that he could get possession of at all likely to be persuaded to live in this country. He studied soil and climate throughout the known world—physical geography in fact—in order to introduce vegetable productions useful in commerce or medicine, if not into England, into other lands more congenial to their constitution and habits. But he was not a traveller, his collecting was done by deputy. He had never been accustomed to accept payment from the poor; a bachelor, he was unfettered by feelings of family duty in indulging his compassionate instincts. And he found abundant opportunities for their exercise. It was a time of war; so unfortunately is this; but the wars of a century ago, some of which he did his utmost to prevent, were with our relatives and neighbours, and their effects were more immediately apparent in his own circle. Many families whom he had attended in affluence he continued to prescribe for in their poverty, and not unfrequently contrived, whilst feeling a pulse at his farewell visit, to slip a bank-note into the hand of his patient as a parting prescription.

Another class from whom he refused payment was that

of seafaring men. Many of this class consulted him, and to them he always said, in his concise manner, "Bring me plants, I prefer plants to money." So they brought him plants from all quarters of the globe, and described the places where they were found, how they were growing, and in what soil. Thus he received catalpas, kalmias, magnolias, firs, oaks, and maples from America, transplanting, in return, teas to the southern part of that continent, bamboos to Jamaica, and spices of various kinds to countries suitable for their growth. Mindful also of his own wants, he gave much attention to the cultivation of Turkey rhubarb and of the cinchona, from which we derive Peruvian bark, and our modern preparation of it—quinine, besides sundry other medical shrubs and trees. We must not, however, linger in the garden.

If the "man who makes two blades of grass grow where only one grew before is a benefactor to mankind," surely we may give that title to our honoured friend John Fothergill.

Lest the specimens brought to Upton should die, and the remembrance of them be lost, he employed several artists to copy them as they flowered or reached perfection, and his portfolios contained many thousand illustrations. I am sorry to say this valuable collection of drawings is no longer in England,—having been purchased at the death of its owner by the Empress Catherine of Russia, to whom the Doctor's name was well known. She gave for it £2300.

We must not be tempted to dwell too long on the many-sided character of this noble man, but proceed to speak of the undertaking that turned his thoughts towards education. He had a wonderful power of doing a great deal in a little time, and a talent for seeing the right thing to be done and the right man to do it, if not able to accomplish it himself. He would have been a good administrator in any department. He gave the first impetus to numerous sanitary measures and improvements in London, and his known eminence in that line led to his being requested by Government to give advice about the gaol fevers which were so terrible and uncontrollable. In pursuit of this duty, accompanied by John Howard, the philanthropist, he visited the prisons of the metropolis, and beheld with his own eyes the evils of the existing system with which we are familiar from report. He saw, too, that even with the best regulations little could be done for those grown up in crime; they were hardened in wickedness. But, while as the physician he was obliged to confess that little could be cured, he saw at the same time that much evil might be prevented by an early and better training of the children. It has been the universal, ever-recurring cry of the thoughtful in all ages—"Give us the education of the young while they are pliable and impressionable!" Their training—not merely their instruction—but their education in its fullest sense.

True to the Society of which he was a respected member, his first thought was of Friends. What was the state of education amongst them? Was it, as it ought to be, an example to be pointed to? In this, as in many other matters, especially in those affecting the welfare of the classes least able to help themselves, Friends were pioneers. Beneath their peculiarities, (which became increasingly peculiar as time progressed and the changes of the world at large left the "Quakers" comparatively unchanged,) there was a foundation of shrewd good sense and executive power.

In the early days of the Society, when fathers and mothers

were often taken from their families, and, because of their religious opinions, thrown into prison for months together, it would not have been surprising if the children's education had suffered. But instead of that, or, perhaps, because of that, the care of the young was one of the first subjects considered as soon as its government was organized. Under the circumstances they felt the advantage of boarding schools for their children, and from time to time such schools were established by their various Quarterly Meetings. This word Meeting has two meanings, the district and the assembly. There are Preparative, Monthly, and Quarterly meetings; the first held once a month in each separate town to *prepare*, the others at the intervals implied by their names, the members in two or three towns uniting for a Monthly, and those in a county or sometimes two counties for a Quarterly meeting. The morning hours of the meeting day are devoted to a "meeting for worship." In the "meeting for discipline" which follows the first business attended to is the answering of the "Queries"—a set of questions respecting the state of the Society, some of which are to be answered at each Preparative meeting, the replies being taken by representatives to the next Monthly meeting.

There the collected replies are condensed, and forwarded, again by representatives, to the Quarterly meeting. These are further condensed for transmission, as before, to the Yearly meeting held in London, in May. The several compilings are operations requiring great nicety, and unbounded patience on the part of the clerk. Alterations suggested in his minutes, when he thought them complete,—one word in place of another, conveying perhaps a shade of different meaning to the proposer's mind, but imperceptible to the general intellect, must, to use a quaker expression, be "very trying." Good discipline for the clerk possibly, but still "trying." We have spoken of the clerk as "he" but one peculiarity of the Society is the separate management of their portion of the business by "Women Friends," giving them an independence and a self-reliance rare in former times.

One of the Queries thus brought month by month to the minds and consciences of this quiet people is "Are the necessities of the poor among you properly inspected and relieved, and is good care taken of the education of their offspring?" From the earliest days the "poor" had received due attention and help so delicately given, that only the few overseers in a meeting and each recipient in his own case have any idea who is helped by the meeting's funds. But, notwithstanding many attempts to keep pace with their educational wants, it was about this time the general feeling that there existed a deficiency of school accommodation for "those not in affluence," as the good Friends carefully put it. There were no National or British Schools, no Board Schools, where children could learn things necessary and unnecessary; poor Friends lived in poor neighbourhoods under many disadvantages and bad influences. Something must be done to remove the children and give them a sound training.

This was the reply to Dr. Fothergill's enquiries, and the deficiency weighed upon his mind. Many plans for supplying it were suggested by one person and another, but abandoned as insufficient or otherwise unsuitable. Our observant and thoughtful friend still held himself ready for prompt action whenever the right plan should appear. At last it came.

He was visiting a gentleman in the north, and there heard incidentally of the unfortunate termination to the experiment at Ackworth. That, notwithstanding repeated advertisements, a fox and her cubs were the only tenants that had applied for admission, and but for the interposition of the Rector the premises would have been already pulled down. As usual with large empty buildings, it was said to be fit for a lunatic asylum or a school.

"Why not for our school?" exclaimed the Doctor, and in spite of objections and difficulties in a very short time he secured the house and 84 acres of land for the sum of £7,000. He did not lay down all the money himself, but he headed a subscription handsomely, the remainder followed, and Ackworth was handed over to the Yearly Meeting the following May as a national boarding school for its members, girls as well as boys. In those days they were treated equally and impartially by the Society.

Friends have a way of serving their community without remuneration, an economical plan of managing their concerns and one ensuring disinterested help. Accepting literally the command "Freely ye have received, freely give," their ministers set the example, and the lower offices of the church and secular appointments are, with trifling exceptions, filled gratuitously. The plan has advantages and disadvantages, but their discussion is not our business. Several of the earliest officers of the new Institution were unpaid volunteers, full of interest in the serious undertaking. They were valuable assistants at first, and when the disadvantages began to show themselves the plan was changed from arbitrary presents to fixed salaries.

The terms for boarders were £8 8s. a year, without extras,

outdoing even Dotheboys Hall. For this the children were to be clothed and fed as well as taught the whole year through from nine years old to fourteen, if so it pleased the parents. The terms were afterwards raised to £10, but at first were only eight guineas. It was, of course, not the full cost, but the rest was made up by a general contribution from all parts of the country. It will scarcely be believed, but is told us as a fact, that a serious protest was sent forth to the effect that to speak of the school as intended for " those not in affluence " and to fix the terms at £8 8s. was a clear contradiction !

To Mary Skelton even it seemed an insurmountable obstacle to her boy's wishes ; though imperceptibly he must have cost her more than that at home, it *was* imperceptibly. Then there was the coach-fare, and though clothing would be supplied as needed at the Institution, he must go creditably furnished with linen at any rate. She slept little the night after Mrs. Dunning had told her news, so simple yet so important to these simple people. But at last the way cleared before her. In the morning she would be going into the town and she would take the opportunity of consulting her friend on Castle Hill.

"Mother art thou going to market in thy better shawl ? " asked the careful little daughter as the mother opened the side door instead of going through the shop as usual.

"Dost thou not see I am Abby ? " was the unsatisfactory reply, that left Abby wondering what would come next.

Miss Lawson, Mary's appreciating friend at once entered into her hopes and difficulties. She remembered one of the many useful little funds for helping their members which was available for such a purpose, and she would answer for her brother's writing to the Superintendent to enquire if there were a second vacancy, but she advised Mary to say nothing about it until they received the reply lest the disappointment, if so it ended, should be greater than the little man could bear.

Mother folded up her "better shawl" in silence on her return home, waiting for the right time to speak, but meanwhile secretly working in preparation for what she hoped would be the announcement to be made.

Letters were costly and slow in 1810. The next "First-day" at meeting Mary looked enquiringly into Miss Lawson's face, but it gave no sign. Monday passed, and Tuesday. On Wednesday she was seen coming down Kilvert Street with an alacrity that promised well for what she had to say. There were no customers in the shop, and John Skelton, sen., was seated in his straight-backed arm-chair in the parlour, knotting together the ends of "thrums," to provide a cheap string for parcel-tying.

"Is Mary at liberty for a few minutes dost thou think, John? I should like to speak with her."

"My wife saw thee coming, Abigail Lawson, and will be here directly. Wilt thou please to take a seat?" said John, adding with quiet humour, "I am doing my best to make ends meet, thou sees."

"I hope thou wilt succeed, John," was all the visitor had time to say before his wife appeared. Miss Lawson hastened to relieve her suspense.

"My brother has heard from the Superintendent, and John may go with Willie Dunning if you can manage it with the help I told thee of, and thou canst have him ready, Mary."

"I will undertake to have him ready," the mother replied

cheerily, " and father here thinks we can find what will be wanted in addition to the sum David Lawson will get for us. We are both of us greatly obliged to thee and thy brother, and I hope the boy will always be grateful to you."

" There is not much to be grateful for, Mary; I hope he will make good use of his opportunities. But I will not hinder thee a moment. Farewell, John, try and make those ends more than meet. A little overlapping is a very comfortable thing thou wouldst find."

CHAPTER III.

Arrival at Ackworth and a day's life there.

So their plans were changed. The boys were not to be separated after all, and Gilbert Dunning did not accompany them to school. Two or three other children, girls as well as boys, were going at the same time, and it was decided that a " Woman Friend " should have charge of the " cargo," as it was called. She looked quite equal to the task, the parents thought, as the little company met at the coach-office in Market Street. She was not personally known to them, but had been visiting in the neighbourhood, and her return to Pontefract fitted in opportunely with the children's departure for school. The whole inside of the coach had been secured, and the party were tightly packed in, along with provisions for the journey to save expense.

Picture to yourselves this " going to school," you luxurious first-class passengers, who get out at every opportunity " to stretch your legs," and who talk of " black Monday " or Thursday, as the case may be, that is to snatch you from

home for a ten weeks' absence! Think of these cramped
little limbs and heavy little hearts, with no prospect of
return for four long years, during which they may hope to
be visited by some member of their family, perhaps once in
each twelve months,—some of them, perhaps, by none at all.
Think of this and be thankful!

It must have been rather a peculiar looking company that
assembled at the coach-office on the morning of their
departure, dressed in whatever was convenient to their
parents to provide, without regard to colour or symmetry,—
the grey duffel cloak and poke bonnet of their caretaker
being the crowning emblems of use before beauty. The
fathers and mothers had gone up with the boys, the brothers
and sisters of both families were standing at the shop door or
looking through the octagon window, for the coach would
come down Kilvert Street, and if all went well, would pass
the Skelton's house. That was the thing—if all went well.

Two mail coaches and four ordinary stages galloped out of
the town by that route each day, and six times a day the
guard's horn was the signal for heads popping up at the
windows to watch if they got safely past the "pump."
Coachmen find it difficult sometimes to pass an inn, but here
the lion in the way was—a pump. One of the many springs
in that part of the town had been thus utilized at the surface,
and very useful it was. The only fault was its position, so
near the middle of the open space, yet so far from the corner
as to be quite out of sight of any one driving down the
Kilvert Street hill until he was close upon it. But a coachman with any spirit *must* drive out of town in good style
whatever the consequences; he *must* gallop down the hill
and trust to good fortune or experience to keep him out of

the danger at the foot. Sometimes the chariot and horses came to grief, often they " swayed over," as the people said, in turning the corner, but righted themselves again. A great amount of strong language was expended on it, but nothing was done. The pump was there before stage-coaches were thought of, when parcels and luggage were conveyed out of town by a string of pack-horses through a narrow lane, and being first on the ground it had a right to it. Common sense prevailed at last however. It was removed to the side of one of the houses, and there it has kept its place long after coaches as well as pack-horses have become things of the past. With this possible danger at the outset of the journey it is no wonder that the little party trembled with excitement as they watched the prancing steeds approach. The boys might not get off after all. They might be upset just at the very door.—No!—Yes!—No! they are safely past, and the watchers may all turn in for a good cry in their several quiet corners.

I dare not undertake to describe the journey; I only know it came to an end at last. One incident has been recorded which leads us to hope that a little, if even grim humour, was discoverable under that drab bonnet to enliven the way for the poor children. At one stage of the journey a gentleman was waiting to ask for an inside place. " Quite full !" growled coachee, " and a queer lot too, a regular tag-rag-and-bobtail." He did not suppose the speech was heard by the inside passengers, and at the end of his stage came obsequiously to the door to beg to be remembered. Our severe-faced friend laid three sixpences on his hand one by one. "That is from Rag, and that from Tag, and that from Bobtail," said she without a smile, and apparently unconscious of sarcasm.

There must have been a deep-springing jet of fun beneath the even surface that weight and pressure were unable to keep entirely down. Only the all-seeing Judge could know how much of sacrifice the subdued demeanour and dull garments cost her. The blessing is that He did know.

It was evening when they arrived at the inn, which was a a sort of appendage to the school, secured with some additional land about ten years after the first purchase. Leaving part of their luggage under the landlord's care, they proceeded with steps tottering from cold and stiffness to the Institution. They went in at a little side-gate, and proceeded between two high walls to the lodge; thence through the great passage, nearly sixty yards long, at this hour dimly lighted by two or three oil lamps. It looked dismal and dreary. The wide empty corridor, with its bare walls and stone floor, echoed their footsteps as they paced along in timid wonder. It was not at all comforting or assuring. But when their guide suddenly opened the door of the housekeeper's room at the end, the aspect of things altered. The blaze of a fire bespeaking the proximity of the "pit's mouth," flashed suddenly upon their dazzled and bewildered sight. The superintendent and housekeeper were waiting to give them a kindly welcome, and a plain but sufficient meal was ready for them, to which, however, they felt scarcely able to do justice. Beds were more to be desired than food in their weary condition. Bidding adieu to their chaperone, who was to pursue her journey home the following day, the girls disappeared into the mysterious "terra incognita" of their own apartments, and the boys were soon asleep in theirs.

No lying in bed next morning, though, to make up for loss

of rest.   Ackworth regulations were Spartan, someone has
said; and he might have added, strongly impressed with the
rule of the Medes and Persians as well.   Fortunately for our
travellers, the hour for rising was still the winter one—
quarter to seven; next month they would be called at six.
After rubbing their eyes, and wondering for a moment where
they were, they discovered themselves to be in a long room
with a row of beds against the wall on each side, and rows
of chests, for clothes, down the centre.   Blue checked
counterpanes, no carpets, no superfluities of any kind.
Standing on the concrete floor, " in their stocking feet,"
while they shuffled on their clothes, they were forcibly
reminded of their absence from home.   But regrets and tears
would have been worse than useless.   The boys were called
to action.   Following their room-companions down the stone
stairs, they came to the passage where their shoes had been
left the night before.   Uncleaned (except once a week, and
then merely oiled) they were quickly resumed, the brass stud
fastening the regular Ackworth shoe being a good contrivance,
as the new-comers saw at once.   Downstairs, again, to the
cellar.   Here they found a twelve-feet-long trough, about
six inches deep and twice that width, at which a row of boys
were washing themselves.   John and Willie arrived just in
time for the clean water.   It was changed when half the
boys had completed that portion of their toilet.   The next
move was to the shed-court, where they joined, as well as they
could, in the peculiar, but no doubt beneficial, custom of
gargling.   Thence they were marched, in military order, to
the schoolrooms, for an hour's study.   The new boys, however, were taken to the " Office" instead, to have their
names and ages duly entered, an inventory made of all their

belongings, and to undergo something of an examination, with a view to fixing their places in class. A pocket-comb was supplied to each, and a piece of whipcord to fasten it to a button. By the time this was done it was eight o'clock, and the bell rang for breakfast—the best meal of the day. But before they could take their seats at table their bodily stature must be ascertained, to fix their places in shed and dining-room. Both "our" boys were found to belong to the third table, where they were soon seated, with a tin can of Ackworth "sops," and a tin or horn spoon to eat them with laid for each on the clothless board.

We read amongst the old minutes of the Committee that in 1797, the superintendent "being of the judgment it may contribute to the children's health, their milk has been given them with less mixture." By 1810 the "mixture" must have been further reduced, and the milk given pure and good, for Ackworth porridge dwells very pleasantly in the remembrance of all the old Ackworth scholars we have heard speak of it. Nothing has tasted so good since. It has sometimes occurred to me that if the old appetite could return, wives and cooks might have a better chance of equalling the compound, but it may be treasonable to suggest the idea. After breakfast to the playground for half an hour's play or to the gardens for mimic work. The gardens were outside the "shed-court" divided from it by a wall. They were favorite places of resort for a certain class of boys and were quite models of ingenuity. Here might be seen a garden-house built of clay with windows of glass, and doors that would open and shut; there a canal made lively with minnows, or a lake with its banks ornamented by miniature willows and water-plants. At that time it was one of the most useful corners of the Institution.

Nine o'clock to twelve were school hours. They were passed by John and Willie in the writing-room, the front one looking over the playground, where "Master Joseph" held sway in his own peculiar manner. He had been there from the commencement—was indeed the only master at first; but two months after the opening, we read in the minutes, that "J. Donbavond" (that was his proper name) "has already more scholars than he can do with," and an assistant is appointed at a salary of £10, Joseph himself receiving at that time just double the sum. He was a fine looking man who wrote like copperplate and "was as good a swimmer as a penman," rhythm and regularity tending to perfection in both strokes. "His favourite humour was to do a kind act with an air of severity." "Get away with thee," he was heard to say with an emphatic elbow-jerk to a very little boy sent to him to be caned, "*thee* be caned! why thou art a coward! thou art afraid to go into the bath! Get away with thee!" So says of him the late William Howitt, who had been a pupil at Ackworth some six or eight years before our little friends, and who has told sundry amusing tales of the doings there.

The unwilling candidates for a birching did not often meet with so welcome a rebuff, though. If he thought a boy deserved correction and could bear it, Joseph Donbavond was not the man to flinch from his duty. "Now then for *Jee tu preparee!*" he used to say, taking a pinch of snuff with his usual three taps on the box-lid, and his peculiar turn of the elbow; "I'll give thee *Jee tu preparee!*" But what meaning he connected with his formula no one ever knew. Various suggestions were made by his irreverent pupils at the time and since, but whether it was an order to prepare which he supposed he was giving in French, or a hidden allusion to the "peppering" in store for the unlucky wight, no philologist amongst them has been able to discover.

Master Joseph was now the writing master. Half the boys were under his care in the morning, the other half in the afternoon, each day. No wonder they turned out good writers! After school there was another half-hour's play before dinner. Again the preparatory assembling in the "shed" in double row, according to height, and again the marching to the dining-room, smallest boys first, the two lines separating as they reached the tables, and passing, still keeping step, to their seats. · All being seated, there was a sudden and complete silence for a few moments, that each might, in his own heart, thank the Giver of all good things "for what he was about to receive"—the Quaker's silent grace. A movement of the master's foot upon the sanded floor announced the commencement of business, and the carvers set to work in good earnest. The work was not heavy to-day. The new-comers were unlucky ; it was Tuesday, and a pudding day, which meant pudding instead of, not in addition to, meat and vegetables. "Third day's" pudding was boiled suet with treacle. The day before had been hot meat, to-morrow there would be "Lobscouse," a sort of resurrection dish that had a medium character amongst the boys. "Fifth day," meeting day, there would be again a pudding dinner, and one universally detested. "Baked batter" was its name in the cookery book; "Clatty vengeance" in the children's vocabulary—a suggestive nickname. On "Sixth day" they would have hot meat, roast or boiled, the remains appearing the following day in the shape of Lobscouse again. "First day" had advantages of

its own. It was the only dinner susceptible of variation.
When gooseberries were in season it was gooseberry pie.
The pies were made in round tin dishes nearly a foot and a
half in diameter, with a bottom crust as well as a top, a
good substantial dish. When apples were ready they were
used for the pies, and between the gooseberry and apple
seasons rice cheesecakes, as they were called, had their turn—
cold, baked rice puddings, spotted with the old-fashioned
Smyrna raisins. Forty-eight of these pies or puddings
were baked every week for the two dining-rooms, dividing
into goodly portions amongst the three hundred children.
They had plenty to eat at dinner-time. Wooden trenchers
served them instead of plates, an excellent substitute when
the trenchers were good and whole; but what was to be
done when time and hot water had cracked them, and the
gravy and sauce ran through on to the well-scrubbed tables?
John and Willie looked round for an answer, and soon
learned the Ackworth plan of filling up the cracks—a novel
use for pudding and potatoes. Cans of very small beer furnished their beverage.

After dinner came another half-hour's play; and at two
o'clock, on re-assembling, our boys were sent to the
reading-school at the bottom of the colonnade. Here they
found the reading-master, William Doubleday,

> " A man of countenance serene,
> " True index of his mind,
> " Where all, whatever it *had* been,
> " Was now to peace resigned."

Like " Master Joseph " he was a fine-looking man, erect
and dignified, and like him with hair combed straight back
and cut at the neck, like a girl's. The style suited both

faces remarkably well, showing their noble foreheads to great advantage. These two masters were married, and lived in the village. There were two other masters and four apprentices on the boys' side, and a similar number of teachers and apprentices for the girls; but of their wing, I am sorry to say, I have little knowledge. Afternoon school lasted till five, when there was a further instalment of play, followed by supper at six. Supper was unsatisfactory. It generally consisted of bread and butter, occasionally of bread and cheese, and water. A lump of butter was dabbed in the middle of a thick slice of bread and covered by another slice as thick. That was the allowance. If a boy possessed a pocket-knife so much the better; if not he had to spread the butter as best he could—often, I dare say, by " rule of thumb." Two quart cans of water started their rounds from the same end. No. 1, after drinking, passed his can to No. 3, and he to No. 5. No. 2, in like manner, passed the second can to No. 4, who gave it to No. 6, and so on round the table. Some advantage in the plan was no doubt apparent to the authorities behind the scenes, for they were particularly clever in attending to details and in busying themselves with minutiæ, but so far it is hidden from the present generation. Supper was soon despatched—too soon, in fact, for no further supply could be obtained, and it was to satisfy the young appetites until eight o'clock next morning. After supper the boys were expected to spend an hour in preparing lessons. The school-rooms were warmed by means of hot-air pipes; but as these were carried round the upper part of the walls, while the floors were flagged, and, of course, without cover, the effect was the reverse of that generally desired, and it was often with hot heads and cold feet, that the boys turned out at eight o'clock and assembled once more in the shed, this time for their " Roll Call." The long list of names having been gone through, the boys next proceeded to the dining-room for " Reading." A chapter in the Bible was read to them by a master each evening before they retired to rest, Sunday evening only excepted, and then the programme was pleasantly enlarged. It was the one time in the week when the whole family were assembled together, boys and girls, masters and mistresses all gathering in the boys' dining-room. After the chapter read by a master as usual, one of the first-class-boys read a selected portion of Scripture; he was followed by a first-class-girl, and she by one of the mistresses. It is a good old custom still kept up.

Dr. Fothergill proposed that the pupils on both sides the house should be taught a trade. It was one of his favourite ideas that " Learning and labour, properly intermixed, greatly assist the end of both—a sound mind in a healthy body." But it was never carried into practice. It never seemed possible to meet with the knowledge of a trade and suitable companionship for the children together. They were all in turn called upon to take part in household duties, boys as well as girls; but that was the nearest approach to realizing the good Doctor's theory. The boys cleaned the knives and forks and shoes of the establishment, and the girls repaired all the linen, except that, on " Fourth day afternoons," a party of boys went to the Matron's room to darn stockings and " run them at the heels." There was a little feeling of jealousy about this : they cleaned *all* the girls' shoes, and, moreover, cleaned them with blacking, while theirs were only oiled, and they thought the girls might have darned *all* the stockings. We seldom like what is good for us. More than one "old boy," I fancy, has found that needle-practice useful to him in after years, and their oiled shoes were really blessings in disguise. What would the state of their feet have been without the wet-excluding oil? The boys helped also in the bakehouse and dairy, the garden, and farm; to wait at table, and turn the mangle; always rewarded, if well-behaved, by a hot cake, a few apples or gooseberries, or a well-buttered crust.

There were worse places than Ackworth even in those days.

CHAPTER IV.

Further experiences at Ackworth, agreeable and otherwise.

Pupils intended for teachers often remained at Ackworth as apprentices from the age of fourteen to that of twenty-one, afterwards rising, if there was a vacancy, to the post of master. During the whole seven years the length of holiday allowed to an apprentice was four weeks. A master could have two weeks in each year. It was a greater strain than many of the youths could bear; in some the physical health, in others the brain, gave way, and to all it was an enervating life, and an inadequate preparation for their future responsibilities in the school. From ignorance of the progress in the great world, comparing themselves only with themselves, the authorities of the out-of-the-way little world at Ackworth considered themselves perfect. They endeavoured to stand still, to remain as they were; but that being impossible, they ended in slipping backwards.

The " notions of discipline were traditional," someone has said; they were often cruel, and the determination to bring offenders to justice frequently led to a perversion of it. The idea of our police detectives that the end justifies the means took possession of those in command at Ackworth, with but little exception, about this period. They seemed to think of punishment not as a necessary regulation for the improvement of the delinquent and the protection of society, but as a personal matter between master and boy; and, like detectives, they did not scruple to use " dodges " which would have been thought deserving of censure and contempt if practised by the children. It was in fact a contest of ingenuity.

And yet it is evident there was a desire to prevent the administering of severe punishment in the heat of personal feeling. A " birching " was not allowed to be given " there and then and have done with it," as children prefer it when inevitable. The master was checked, and, we may add, the punishment increased by delay in its carrying out. One plan was for the culprit to be brought down to a " Master's Meeting " after the other boys were in bed, and there to receive the reward of his sins. It often did not amount to much,—two strokes on each hand and four on the back, but the mystery and solemnity made it awful. Another plan was the institution of a " Caning-book." There must be at least one witness present, who must sign his name to a statement when, by whom, and why, the caning was inflicted; the book to be produced at the next master's meeting, and its records commented on. What more could be done? In the absence of the preventive help of full and varied occupation in play-hours how could discipline be maintained except

by corporal punishment? That it was outward discipline
only, that within lay "smouldering discontent" and dogged
obstinacy, was not the less a natural consequence.

But these are bygone times. The arrangement of scholar,
apprentice, master in unbroken succession accounts for much
that needed altering at one period, and that has long been
altered, thanks to the influence of outside elements, which at
last gained admission. It is interesting, however, and pro-
fitable sometimes to look back and compare our advantages
with those of our forefathers, asking ourselves at the same
time, "Can we with equal satisfaction compare the results?"

The only official who in those early days raised his voice
against the hard treatment of the children, and particularly
against the caning, was Wm. Doubleday, the reading-master.
His feelings were strong about it. He used to ask—

> "If with Solomon I whip,
> "Why not with Moses stone?"

maintaining that they belonged equally to the old dispen-
sation. It was a belief more pleasing to his pupils than to
his colleagues. The kind-hearted superintendent sympa-
thised with him to a certain extent, but the censure implied
by his actions, even when he did not speak his mind, was an
uncomfortable feeling for his fellow-teachers. He was simply
in advance of the age in that particular, for we must remember that the severity spoken of at Ackworth was only in
accordance with the spirit of government outside that micro-
cosm—the spirit that made a man's life the forfeit for quite
trifling offences. But sunshine was ever more powerful
than an easterly wind. Wm. Doubleday's pupils gave him
little trouble; they appreciated his justice and mild firmness,
and they felt relieved by the absence of that irritating spirit

of irony so prevalent in the manner of some of the other teachers. Just then it was the tone of the school. The very name given to the places of solitary confinement—Light and Airies—I had always considered to be ironical, bitterly so; but I have been corrected by an "old boy" who says he ought to know, for he was once confined there four weeks! and he maintains that they were literally both light and airy. The windows were not out of reach, and they were a good size, but being painted outside they were useless as places of amusement, and they were padlocked.

In one of the three rooms a prisoner had managed to rush up before his jailer, slip his hand through the open window, and scratch a tiny place on the paint outside, giving a most welcome peep into the outer world, but there was no chance of communicating with it. The bakehouse was underneath, and pipes for the conveyance of hot air were brought from behind the oven into these prison-rooms; but somehow or other they did not work, and the air that entered, though there was plenty of it, was most frequently cold. Light and airy was really no misnomer. A boy in disgrace was turned into his cell at 6 a.m. and fetched back to bed at 10 p.m. His pockets were searched each morning before he went in. A chair and table were provided for his use, with a Bible, and sometimes an Ackworth spelling-book. The food brought to him was like that of the other boys, but less in quantity. Such was life in a Light and Airy, stolidly submitted to for even six and seven weeks by some persistent spirits whose endurance was worthy of a better cause.

The famous Ackworth Vocabulary just now alluded to was compiled for the use of the school by Dr. Binns, the third Superintendent. It was used in season and out of season. Besides being allowed to relieve the monotony of solitary confinement, it was the only exception to the strict rule of "books of a religious tendency" to be read on " First day." Why, we do not know; but we do know that Ackworth scholars were good spellers as well as good writers. They were also good readers, and were well practised in the common rules of arithmetic. Little else was taught at first, but these subjects were thoroughly taught, the instruction being greatly in advance of that obtainable by any similar class outside the Society. It attracted numbers who did not properly belong to the section of their body for whom the school was first intended, and many gladly paid the full cost of their children for the sake of so good a foundation in essential knowledge which could be added to later, according to their leisure and requirements.

Our boys had not exhausted their new sensations and experiences at the end of the first day. There was still the bath to be tried for one thing. They had heard terrible accounts of "The Bath," which was, in fact, a cold chalybeate spring nearly a mile distant from the school. It was used three mornings of the week by the boys and three by the girls. The fifty or sixty boys whose turn it was to bathe next morning, John and Willie amongst them, were called between five and half-past and marched off. It was a sharp frosty morning, such as we often have at the end of April, and the walk was just long enough to warm them. The bath they found was about twelve feet square, with a path on three sides, and a wall surrounding it. A second square was covered in for a dressing-room, but it was only used by the girls. The boys undressed just outside the wall, and often had to lay their clothes upon the snow. A flight of steps at the entrance corner led down into the bath, and a large tub was fixed by them or by the jumping board at the other end, in which a master stood to help the boys in. The help was given in a very summary manner. Little boys and new boys were expected to jump from the side, and be caught by the older ones already in the bath ; but if a boy hesitated he was seized by a leg and an arm and tossed in, whatever his terror or dread of the water. So John and Willie had been told, and they had also been told that the boys in the bath did not always catch, and that sometimes they caught and would not let go, holding a little head under water to the verge of suffocation. It was fearful they felt as they looked down into the red abyss. Yet to go voluntarily was better than to be thrown in, and nothing but a cold was to be gained by delaying. First Willie disappeared and then John. No one seemed to be looking out when Willie jumped, and he floundered about a little stunned by striking the water. A hand was soon stretched out for his help, however, and seeing his comrade safely caught, he ducked, and they scrambled out together, delighted to find it not so bad as they expected. No towels, but a run to dry themselves, and they dressed all in a glow. *They* learned to enjoy it, but it was too much for the weaker ones, and no doubt many were injured by it. A crust of bread would have been very welcome after the early rising, but none was offered. An hour's spelling, as usual, before breakfast, instead !

There were not two opinions about their next experience of Ackworth doings. Everyone, whether he could do much or little, liked skipping, and the Ackworth skipping was something wonderful—quite an institution. The rope used was peculiar to the place, but when invented or by whom I never heard. A centre piece of whip-cord was fastened to two lengths of tarred rope and these again to two lengths of whip-cord which were threaded through the handles, thus making a rope of five pieces. This was the short rope, the long rope was an ordinary one about thirty feet long and would allow of twenty boys skipping in it together. Follow my leader, of course, they played in it, and the leader set them some difficult tasks. Sometimes he jumped on his knees, at others he would lie down between the jumps, again, he would take quite a run round and return to the rope at the exact moment of its touching the ground, or he would take his short rope and make it keep time with the long one jumping over both at once. The figure of eight was thought very easy and only worthy of beginners. About the short rope skippers there are equally marvellous tales. Single skipping, that is the rope passed once under the feet at each spring, became difficult from its slowness to some of the more advanced; double, and crossing, and thribble, were the ordinary steps. A few could manage four turns of the rope in one spring and one boy accomplished it twice in succession, which was a great feat. Sixty-four turns of thribble skipping are the greatest number on record, I believe.

An "old scholar" who, as a man, was remarkable for the number of languages he knew and could teach, and, while still a boy, for his command of English, wrote, at the age of twelve, a few lines about this thribble skipping, which, though probably well known to all Ackworth girls and boys, are worth copying as a specimen of juvenile talent:—

" Aloof from these the dexterous skipper bounds,
And lifts his slender form, and thrice revolves
The cord, ere on his feet again he lights :—
As if a friendly cloud sustained his frame,
Or grosser atmosphere kindly upheld him :
And then he sinks, and rising gracefully,
The self same round keeps on, until his blood
Revolves a brisker current in his veins ;
With emulation now his visage glows ;
And as again he rises, and again,
He feels the pride of conscious excellence
Thrill in his heart, and on his fellows looks
With smiles of skill superior."

Neither of our boys obtained any great proficiency in the art, though they became good average skippers, but were never so enthusiastic, for instance, as to deny themselves sufficient dinner for the sake of excelling in skipping afterwards, which a few heads of the profession have been known to do.

Spring came quickly on, the little gardens were sources of increasing interest, days were longer and brighter, and the children began to talk about the General Meeting, and to prepare for the examination which annually takes place then. Some of them expected to see their friends, others hoped for it, but the greater number only wished it were possible. Many of them came from the South of England, and travelling was difficult and expensive. John and Willie had been at school so short a time they were sure no one would come to see them. But they looked forward to the gala time along with the others, for if nothing else fell to their share there would be a good dinner of lamb and green peas, they were told, on both days; and what boy is indifferent to the prospect of an unusually good dinner?

The only difficulty would be the eating of it, and this they found to be true when the time arrived. The boys' dining-room was given up to the landlord of the inn for the accommodation of his guests, and the boys dined in the girls' apartment after its rightful occupants had finished. But there was not room for them to sit down, and they stood tightly packed round the table, eyeing their trenchers full of unwonted dainties, and speculating how much they could secure.

I suppose we have all seen or heard of the forks of that period; forks of two prongs, fine and wide spread. What chance had the poor pinioned boys of landing their peas safely where they were so much desired? They could only "spear" two at once however well they aimed. A more tantalizing dinner could scarcely have been devised. There was not elbow-room for lifting the trencher to a level with the mouth, so the reverse was the only course. One after another, in different parts of the room, according to the position of the master's back, you might see a boy suddenly kneel on the floor and hastily sweep a handful of peas into his mouth, then up again, hoping for another chance of finishing them. Unless they had been far-seeing enough to pocket a breakfast-spoon, what else could they do?

Good dinners are apt to remind us of the "Apothecary's Shop." That was the name of the apartment at Ackworth where the nurse was to be found at a certain hour each evening waiting to attend to patients. It was situated in a small passage leading from the long one to a back entrance, and the door of the master's study was exactly opposite. This was a great resource for nurse. If a boy disputed her authority, "I'll have thee flogged" was sufficient to subdue him at once, for he knew she had only to walk across the passage and the preliminary steps would literally be taken for carrying her threat into effect. Her practice was very simple. "For every evil under the sun"—except chilblains —she had two remedies. Horehound tea for coughs and colds, and solution (Glauber's salts) for the rest. For chilblains there were turpentine if unbroken, and blue lint (lint dipped in blue vitriol) for the very bad broken ones. Poor fellows! There was to be no nonsense about chilblains; John found that out the first winter he was there. Nurse seemed to think boys could help having them, and that they deserved punishment rather than sympathy. John's were broken, but had only needed a plaister, which he came to have renewed, and was very carefully removing the old one, when, catching sight of him she reached forward her hand to expedite matters.

"Oh! please I can do it myself," whimpered John, not accustomed to such rough treatment.

"Do it thyself, can thou? Very well, if thou can do without me, thou had better go!" and, suiting her actions to her words, she gathered up his shoes and stockings, threw them into the passage, and bundled John after them head first. We may be sure he did not trouble her again, however lame he was.

Willie's experience was of a different kind. There was often great difficulty about the water supply. Just outside the boys' colonnade, by the middle column, was a semi-circular stone trough with a tap over it, which ought always to have been available for the boys' use. Sometimes the supply of water was really deficient, but more frequently it was John Pilmore's patience in pumping that ran short and caused so much discomfort to the children.

Half-way down the flags stood a pump, but it was kept locked, and only in very dry weather the boys were allowed to water their gardens from it. The water was not considered suitable for drinking. The day had been very hot, and poor Willie was in a state of distress. No water was to be had, and he was so thirsty he thought Horehound tea would be better than nothing; he had never tasted it, but he would try.

At the proper time he went to the Apothecary's shop for some "medicine for a cold." Nurse looked at him rather suspiciously, but handed him his dose in the usual old-fashioned china cup. Willie took it—and drank it—he could do no other under that stern eye, but he never asked for Horehound tea again, even when he had a cold.

Fortunately there were more agreeable associations with winter than these. The first fall of snow was loudly welcomed by the boys. "Now we shall have treading down!" they exclaimed; and great fun it was. Half-a-dozen rows of thirty boys each, closely packed together, slowly moved across the playground, stamping and treading the snow under their feet into a hard, level skating ground. This was delightful, and so was the skating afterwards, which, however, they called "clogging," and the skates "clogs." They were pieces of wood like a common old-fashioned skate, but with the metal three or four times the usual breadth, and not so deep. Altogether it was a very safe amusement. Then there was sliding. They prepared the "flags" by pouring water down them some frosty night, and next morning had a magnificent slide.

The "flags" was that six-feet broad path, laid down in 1793, from the committee-room door to the garden gate, where brothers and sisters, and cousins, and cousins' cousins, to far-reaching generations, still walk and talk together. It was the only place where boys and girls might associate. The privilege of meeting was lost during sliding time, for the girls had their slide somewhere out of sight. It was a pity, but a necessity, I suppose.

CHAPTER V.

Still Ackworth.—The Reading-master's Daughter.—John's Spelling Lesson, Im-prac-ti-ca-bil-i-ty.

"I want thee to take a message for me to my wife, John," said Wm. Doubleday to our old acquaintance, one afternoon when he had been at Ackworth about six months; and John was nothing loth. Everyone can imagine, I was going to say, the joy of going beyond bounds; but only those can fully realize it who have spent six months in a uniform round of duties almost unbroken by any event, and uncheered by loving words. And it was pleasant to go as a trusted messenger. John felt quite important. If his master could have foreseen all the trouble that was to come of that sending, I wonder if he would have chosen another messenger? I do not know.

John had seen Sarah Doubleday at meeting, and wondered, in his simplicity, as he went along, whether she would open the door herself or whether she kept a servant; and he repeated the message aloud to be sure he remembered it. His knock was answered neither by servant nor mistress, but by a fair, blue-eyed little maiden, a year or two younger than himself, whose

" — hair was thick with many a curl
" That clustered round her head."

She smiled when she saw John, but did not speak. He delivered his message: it was merely concerning the hour of the father's return home in the evening. The sunny little damsel went to the foot of the stairs and called, "Mother!" It was the first word she had spoken, the only word John heard her speak while he remained at Ackworth, but it was sufficient. Her voice was so sweet, her manner so modest, her— in fact, he made up his precocious mind that if ever he had a wife that was to be the one. Of course he did not confess this until long afterwards; but "Mother!" sounded in his ears all the way back to school, and he thought if he could listen to those tones when he came to be a man, life would be full of charm and beauty. Whatever hard work, whatever struggles were before him—and he had seen much of both at home, and looked forward to them as his natural heritage— if that face might be the reward everything would be easy. She (he did not know that her name was Margaret) was not to share the work and the struggles, only the success they were to bring. But he found, alas! on turning in at the gate, that he was still just a schoolboy, with a long column of spelling to learn, and no time for romance. Columns of spelling, even of six and seven syllabled words, with their meanings, were not at all the sort of difficulty he had been dreaming of surmounting on his road to eminence. It was decidedly a coming down, and rather distasteful. He remembered, however, one of his mother's lessons, to do first the work nearest to you, and it would prove the stepping-stone to something beyond; and he wisely decided to grapple with the difficulties of his lesson, leaving the future to "take care of itself."

Im-prac-ti-ca-bil-i-ty was the first word of his column. He learned to spell it, but refused to accept it as a suggestion or an omen; in fact, he would have liked to cross it out of the spelling-book altogether. It was a word that never found favour with him to the end of his life.

He was not sent again to the cottage. He wished " she " were in the school; he could at least have seen her in the distance on the girls' green, or he might have discovered some relationship that would give them a right to go on "the flags." But she could not be spared to attend the school.

In their occasional walks to the common the boys passed the cottage door, and he never failed to look for his " ray of sunshine " as they went by, seldom being disappointed of a bright little gleam. Margaret had the charge of a little brother about a year and a half old, and in that quiet place the procession was too important an amusement to be missed. The "hum of 180 voices " announced its approach, and the young nurse and nursling were almost sure to be at the window; indeed, I am inclined to think she, too, sought a certain face, for one day she pointed out to her mother " the little boy father sent down with a message."

What a comical row of figures they must have looked as they filed past, with their long-tailed coats and leather breeches, coloured stockings and studded shoes, and their hair close-cropped, except a fringe in front hanging straight over their foreheads!

A pair or two of the leather garments were kept to be worn as a punishment for inked or damaged trousers long after they were abandoned for general use. This peculiar dress was no doubt retained longer than it otherwise would have been with an idea, shared by the authorities of some other large schools, that the boys could be known to everybody in the neighbourhood, and brought back if, in desperation at their monotonous lives, some of the more adventurous got into mischief or tried to run away. They did make the experiment not unfrequently, but seldom got further than Wakefield, their appearance betraying them. The dress of the girls also became a sort of uniform, not intentionally in either case; but as both boys and girls were provided with clothes by the institution, it was more convenient and economical to buy large quantities of material and make up the garments of various kinds by an unvarying pattern. They were uniform in another matter, too—winter and summer they wore the same thick dresses. What would keep out the cold would keep out the heat!

The boys were even more grotesque in their walking costume than when out of doors at play. As soon as the inventory of their possessions was taken when they first entered the school they lost sight of the hats or caps in which they had travelled, such coverings not being required for daily use; but when the bell rang "to collect for a walk" they re-appeared, in what manner our friend, Wm. Howitt, will describe better than I. "They (the boys) drew up in two long lines facing each other, perhaps two yards apart. Large wicker baskets were brought forth from a store-room, piled with hats of all imaginable shapes and species, for they were such as had been left by the boys from the commencement of the institution. They wear none except on these excursions; and here they were, broad brims, narrow brims, brown, black, and white, pudding crowns, square crowns, and even sugar-loaf crowns, such as Guy Fawkes wore."

Boys and monitors were agreed in choosing the most unlikely and unsuitable in size possible.

"That's the one for thee," a monitor would say as he bonnetted a little fellow or perched a small sized sugar-loaf on the head of one of the tallest boys. And for once, as our friend says, boys and monitors pulled together. Thus arrayed they proceeded, two and two, with teachers interspersed, to the common, where the command to "spread" was the signal for one of the most enjoyable times in the year.

On their way to the common one memorable afternoon, John was puzzled. Something had happened to "*his* face." He saw, as he passed the cottage, that the baby boy was there, clapping his little hands as usual, and at first John disappointedly thought some other sister or care-taker was with the child, but a second look convinced him there was no change except in the face itself. But what *was* the change? What was the matter? Something must have happened, certainly something was gone. He pondered over it in silence, for he had kept his secret even from Willie, but could not solve the riddle; and not until years afterwards did he learn the facts.

What had really happened was this.

A Friend from Pontefract called upon Mrs. Doubleday one morning, and without apology or preamble proceeded to fulfil her mission.

"Sarah, I am very much surprised that thou allowest thy eldest daughter to curl her hair!"

Friends were accustomed to the interference of elders and overseers in their private affairs. A young small community almost always drifts into this practice. The leaders are strongly impressed with the importance of their views, and jealously watch any act that implies a departure from them or an unsettlement of opinion about them. It was not, therefore, so unusual a speech as it would be now, but it touched Mrs. Doubleday in a tender point. She knew that she did not "allow" her daughter to curl her hair, she had always believed that it curled naturally, but this direct attack opened the door to a suspicion. Could it be possible that the girl so ventured to think and act for herself as to curl it without leave ?

Nothing in the house was supposed to be done without the mistress's knowledge and permission ; but—if this had escaped her vigilance ? She was not going to confess the thought, however, but replied somewhat coolly,

"My daughter does not curl her hair, Hannah Fletcher ; she would not think of such a thing. She would be certain I should not allow it and she could not do it without my knowledge."

"I would not have thee too sure that thou knowest everything that goes on, Sarah," said Hannah Fletcher, and the tone, more than the words, implied that *she* believed in the curl-papers.

"We will have her in," replied the mother in her sharp decided way and going to the door she called "Margaret, I want thee here."

Margaret came.

"Ask her thyself, Hannah Fletcher, I will have nothing to do with it."

"My dear," said the visitor to the astonished girl, "some of thy friends are concerned at the appearance of thy hair. They are afraid thou art tempted to put it in paper."

"I do nothing of the kind, Hannah Fletcher."

There were a few moments of silence The Friend could scarcely repeat the accusation after these denials, but it was evident she was not convinced. Her

"— thoughts congealed into lines on her face, as the vapours
"Freeze in fantastic shapes on the window-panes in the winter."

Margaret quietly undid the scissors that hung along with a pincushion by her side, and handed them to Mrs. Fletcher, with the words, "If thou does not believe me thou may cut them off," meaning the obnoxious curls. Her mother had said she would "have nothing to do with it," but surely she could not allow that to pass unopposed. She remained perfectly inactive, however, though secretly wondering "if Hannah would have the conscience to do it."

Hannah took the scissors, laid her hand on the intractable hair, selected a curl that fell over Margaret's forehead, and—cut. The girl did not move. Another curl went, another, and yet another, from about the face that still looked fair, though shorn.

"There, my dear, that is better," said the operator, as she returned the scissors.

"I am glad thou art satisfied, Hannah Fletcher. The same Hand that curled it before will curl it again, thou wilt see."

It was not like her to act in such a manner; I do not know where she found the courage to do it, nor what she thought of it all when she looked at herself in the glass. I have heard her spoken of as "meek, unmoved," and it was a good description. She had been meek hitherto because she had not been tried, and was not herself conscious of the latent fire beneath the surface. Her mother had never appreciated her so much as on that morning, when she showed unmistakably "whose daughter she was." How she might admire the same spirit opposed to her own wishes was another matter. At present her feelings were complacent. She and her husband were "convinced Friends," and, as is often the case, she, at least, went somewhat to an extreme in carrying out her new views. She placed no value on a pleasing exterior; indeed, she rather distrusted it as a waste of time somewhere; therefore, her daughter's altered appearance was no trouble to her, and did not interfere with her self-congratulation that she had not "been caught napping."

The girl's words came true: as the hair grew again it curled better than ever. It was an ornament that she had until then accepted as a matter of course, but this incident had given an undue value to it. As a check upon vanity Hannah Fletcher's mission proved a failure; not that Margaret was ever vain, but she certainly thought more about her hair after it was cut than ever before. But Hannah Fletcher herself *was* very well satisfied, as Margaret suggested. She had done her duty; she had protested emphatically against the outward adorning of plaiting the hair, and she hoped there was evidence in the dear girl of the meek and quiet spirit that, we are told, is so much more to be desired. We cannot but respect her for doing what she believed to be right, even to the point of risking the displeasure of persons she really liked and esteemed, but she was grievously mistaken as to the true effect of her interference.

This had happened not long before the walk in question, and accounted for the unusual appearance of the face that John so much admired.

A remarkable event occurred in the neighbourhood of

Ackworth this year. A splendid Aloe flowered in the conservatory at Nostell Priory, a fine old place belonging to the Winn family, three or four miles from the school, on the Wakefield road. The Aloe was of the kind popularly supposed to flower only once in a hundred years, and the children were invited to go over and see it. The Sir Roland Winn, whom we hear of being so much interested in watching the Ackworth children at dinner, was the third of his name; he was High Sheriff of the county of York in 1799, and died unmarried in 1805. The estates and the title then unfortunately parted company; the title went to his cousin Edmund Mark Winn, Esq., of Acton, and the family estates to his nephew, John Williamson, Esq., who afterwards obtained a licence to bear the name and arms of Winn. This was the gentleman who kindly invited the children from Ackworth to pay a visit to his conservatory. It was a wonderful treat. The girls went one day and the boys the next. Their first object, of course, was to look at the flower, which they found had grown so tremendously that part of the conservatory roof had been removed, and a square glass tower added to accommodate it. And there it was, towering above them with its magnificent spike of cream-coloured flowers, the beautiful bells so overflowing with honey that the floor of the conservatory all round the plant was covered with the luscious drops. There is no rose without a thorn, and no such store of honey without wasps and bees, as many of the young visitors found that afternoon to their sorrow.

When they had sufficiently admired the Aloe, they were summoned to the lawn; and, as they stood there in a wide semi-circle in front of the house, each of them was regaled with a bun and a horn of ale, besides an apple to put in his pocket. I hope they were allowed to relieve their minds by a good cheer, but it is doubtful. The apples were of such a size that few of the pockets would hold them, and most of them were stowed away elsewhere long before the boys reached home. It was a delightful excursion, notwithstanding the stings.

There was still another gala-day this year, to commemorate an event almost as rare as the flowering of the Aloe itself—the marriage of the superintendent. He was a kindly man and a general favourite. The master who could receive the contents of a plate of oatmeal porridge on his head, as he stood under the nursery window, with the simple remark, as he looked up to see who sent it, "Thou had better be more careful next time thou does that, and look out first," was sure to be a favourite, and I have no doubt the congratulations and rejoicings were hearty and sincere.

Two apple trees were planted on the occasion, one on each side of the garden gate at the end of "the flags." The trees being placed and everything ready, each boy threw a spadeful of earth on the roots of one, and each girl on the roots of the other.

The apple trees are flourishing yet, but how many of the young gardeners could now be found, and where?

CHAPTER VI.

The Return Home. — Perplexities of various kinds. — Hallam. — Heatherby.

Two years of this school life brought our boys to the age of fourteen, the period for leaving Ackworth. Children of their class were generally apprenticed at that age; a longer time spent in "learning," their friends thought, only unfitted them for manual labour. And indeed they ought then to have acquired all that was ordinarily within their reach in the way of learning. Those who were fortunate enough to be sent to Ackworth—I think we may fairly place it before the other schools of the kind—had been thoroughly drilled in the "three Rs," and in spelling. What more could they want? Men and women who could read, write and spell well, who could keep accounts correctly and check promptly their tradesmen's bills, possessed powers greatly in advance of those to be gained generally by people "not in affluence." They were supplied with a good set of tools to begin life with and many of them carved their way to fortune. What would our two do with them, what was their future to be?

John had a desire to be a teacher, and he would have felt no objection to remain at Ackworth as apprentice. Knowing his secret we shall not be at a loss to account for the wish, but it was over-ruled by his parents as they thought it best for him to return with Willie who was to go into a land-surveyor's office in Hallam. So they received a little parting advice, shook hands with their particular friends and once more set out on a journey together. The coach they travelled by stopped to set them down at the Skelton's shop door. Gilbert Dunning was waiting for Willie and taking up his small trunk hurried him off to Friargate where his mother was anxiously looking out for him. Joyful meetings in both houses we may be sure ensued, yet they were not unmixed with surprise and somewhat of dismay. Of course the boys had grown out of the clothes they had taken with them and having been supplied with garments of the institution pattern, their appearance was so altered they were scarcely recognisable. Indeed little Alice Skelton for a long time refused to own the figures in cut-away long-tailed coats and leather shorts as her brother and old playfellow.

Cases are on record of parents and children really not knowing each other after the long unbroken absence at Ackworth. Children had forgotten what father and mother looked like, and parents failed to see in the strong youth of fourteen the little fellow of nine that had left their care. That breaking so entirely the thread of home life was one of the greatest evils of the place. At first it was unavoidable, a necessary evil. Now, happily, it is a past evil and we need say no more about it.

"What Guys they have made of our lads, Mary!" said Mrs. Dunning later in the day.

"Never heed that if they have not made Guys of their minds, Betsy" replied her philosophical friend, "and I do not think they have. The lads can look us frankly in the face which is a great comfort after missing the sight of their faces for two years. They are in good health too, and are growing ever so tall. We can change their coats."

The surprise was not all on the side of the stay-at-home people, however; when John turned from the coach he scarcely knew where he was. The old black door was gone, and so was the octagon window. There were two windows of good white glass instead, and the shop door was between them with "Skelton, Grocer and licensed Tea-dealer" above it in bold black letters. He understood the change then. His mother's plan had been followed, and he was very glad. He did not want to leave the dear old town, though his interest was beginning to wander away from it. The shop

looked beautiful he thought, with a nice mahogany counter
on each side, and a door in one corner opening into the
parlour, for the passage had been laid to the shop.   It was
so snug and comfortable after the immense rooms and long
corridors.

Willie was to have a few weeks holiday before entering
on his apprenticeship at Hallam.   John should have the
same, but what was to be done with him afterwards?   It did
not seem easy to please him.   His old master at the school
in the town, hearing he had been a monitor at Ackworth,
came down to ask if he would help him for a time, and his
father said that was " the very thing."   " For the present,"
mentally added John, " till the right thing turns up."

Willie's holiday soon slipped away, and the friends were
to be parted at last.   They promised each other always to
have a letter on hand ready for a private opportunity, and
if opportunities were too scarce to save up their odd pennies
for postage, which was a serious item then we must
remember.   People paid more for their letters, but they
were certainly better worth having than the " short
communications " that arrive three or four times a day now.
They were more like magazine articles or small newspapers,
and required some reading and thinking about.

A few months after Willie's departure, John found on his
return from school one day at noon, a little commotion in the
shop.   And yet not exactly a commotion, for his mother and
elder sister were standing by with perfect outward composure
while a rough-looking man was helping himself to tea out
of a canister that stood on the counter.   The father was not at
home.   John could not understand it, but they signed to him
to ask no questions.   The man had taken possession of some of

their paper bags, and was putting into one of them great handfuls of tea. He had two bags already filled with black tea in his basket, and now he was adding the green. "Oi dunnot loike th' job," he was saying with each handful, "Oi dunnot loike th' job," but he seemed determined to do "th' job" thoroughly, all the same, whatever it was. When he was satisfied, he put the lid on the canister, took his basket on his arm, gave the women a nod and walked out.

"What does it all mean, Mother?"

"It is a distraint for church rates, John. Friends don't think it right to pay them, and the vicar sends to take something he can sell, and get the money that way. He says he must do it because of those who come after him, but, I believe, many of them would rejoice if the law were altered. If we go against it for conscience sake, thou knows, we must take the consequences and make no opposition. It would have cost us much less to pay the demand at first, it was only about two and fourpence but by this time the expenses for a warrant, and so on, have mounted it up to more than a pound. But there would be no blessing on the money saved by doing wrong."

"He was taking plenty of tea," said John.

"They are not allowed by law to pay a second visit for the same demand, so they generally err on that side. I dare say he had five or six pounds of tea in his basket, but there will be the cost of selling it to add to the warrant. Perhaps he has not taken too much after all."

"It is very strange," said John, " I do not remember their coming before."

"No, for one thing, thou hast been away, and for several

years before that a gentleman paid the church rates and
Easter-dues for all the Friends in the town. We could not
imagine how it was we escaped distraints so long; but
our well-intentioned friend died last year, and then it was
explained. We could not have accepted it had we known
it was being paid, yet it was a relief. Now the robbery,
as some people call it, is beginning again."

"I call it robbery," broke in Abby. "What right have
they to our tea?"

"It is a good plan, Abby, to try to look at things from
our neighbours' point of view as well as our own, especially
if the neighbours are not neighbourly in their behaviour.
They have sometimes more reasons for it than we see from
our side. These church rates and Easter-dues are part of a
system the church people have grown up in and been taught
to think right. They were settled when there were. no
dissenters and everyone was supposed to belong to the
" State church," and as their ministers must live by their
church work, it was only right that everyone should contribute. Now, things are different, and we hope the law
will be changed bye and bye, but meanwhile we cannot pay
the money because we think the true spirit of ministry
being a free gift ought not to be made a merchandise of."

Mrs. Skelton had told her son that the vicar sent to take
something he could sell and thus obtain his money, but this
time the vicar, or the law in his name, found that his
messenger had taken something he could not turn into
money. The man had forgotten that a license was required
for selling tea and he vainly tried to get rid of it. Driven
to despair, in the course of a few days, he returned to the shop
and asked if the Skeltons would allow him to sell his plunder

at their own door, under the protection of their own license! This was rather too much, the strictest disciplinarian could not require that they should voluntarily assist in their own despoiling.

" Even looking at it from the vicar's point of view," Abby said, "so far as she could guess where that point was situated, the request was an impertinence."

" Or the last resource of a man in a difficulty ?" suggested the much-enduring mother.

Abby shook her head, and John said that was "like mother."

But it was not the man's last resource; he improved on his plan the next day. While the family were seated at dinner they heard the shop door open and close again. Abby was quickly in attendance, but could see no one. On looking further, however, she spied by the door the now well-known basket and the three parcels of tea. She seized the treasure, and bore it in triumph to the parlour.

" He has been obliged to bring it back; see, mother! and he has left us the basket too. We are gainers at last."

" Not at last, only for this year, I'm afraid, little woman," said her father, sadly. " Thou may depend upon it they will straighten it up next time."

Abby sighed. It was a very unsatisfactory state of things, she felt; but she would have bemoaned it more strongly than by sighing could she have foreseen that next year the table they were sitting round would be the spoil selected. The father was right; they "straightened it up " in their own fashion, and there was no redress. John wrote an account of the whole transaction to his good friend at Hallam, who was as deeply indignant at " the attempted theft " as if

it were not a common occurrence. Both of them lived not
only to experience such losses themselves many times repeated, but to see the law altered in the name of Justice
towards the increasing number of individuals who were not
ministered to by the " Established Church."

Willie was a capital correspondent, lively and humourous;
and his letters were an immense treat to his more sedate
friend, who was still plodding on at the school, waiting for
he knew not what. Unconsciously—as so many of our acts
are performed, or, rather, in happy unconsciousness of what
their effects will be—at the end of this indignant letter
Willie laid a match to the train so long prepared. " What
does thou think I heard to-day?" he wrote, in a lady-like
postscript. " William Doubleday, our old master, has left
Ackworth, and is going to open a boarding-school here. He
has taken a large old house called Heatherby Hall, about a
mile from Hallam, and he will open school in it after the
midsummer holidays. I shall be quite pleased to see him
again." John responded to the sentiment warmly, but he
substituted " them " for " him " in his own mind. He now
began to see his way. William Doubleday would of course
need help, and, according to the custom of the day, he would
take apprentices. What better master could he himself have
than one with such advanced views on education? And
how fortunate it was that he was free from indentures elsewhere!

Willie was at Hallam, too.

He lost no time in giving form to his ideas. He repre-
sented to his father and mother how much more it would be
to his advantage to pass the years of his apprenticeship in a
high-class private boarding-school than at a small day-school,

however good and respectable. His parents thought him ambitious and were timid. " We cannot tell that William Doubleday wants an apprentice."

" We can find out by asking the question, father; there can be no harm in that."

" Who is to write? I do not know him, and should not like to take the liberty."

" But I know him, father; and if thou will only give me leave I will write to him myself. I think he will remember me; but even if not, he will not be offended at my asking."

Once more Mary had recourse to their kind friends, the Lawsons, who were unhesitatingly on John's side. " Let the boy write," they said.

So the " boy " was allowed to write. Could we see the letter now we should most likely find traced on its old yellow paper long sentences well rounded with expressions of profound respect. That was considered the proper style of letter-writing, and we may be sure John did his best. But copied correspondence is apt to be dry and tedious, as is proved in too many of the biographies we try to read. We will therefore skip this altogether, and briefly say that, when William Doubleday opened school at Heatherby in the following summer, John Skelton was one of his apprentices. The latter used to lament when he had growing-up children of his own that he had been " very naughty" about this going to Hallam, too persistent and too secret as to his n.otive for wishing it.

Who shall judge him? or shall we leave the verdict an open one ?

When the time arrived for entering on his new duties he was, unexpectedly, sorry to go, for his family were in

6

trouble, and he did not like to leave them. But he must be
" punctual in fulfilling his engagements," that is one of the
" Queries," and a " clear answer" could not be sent to the
Monthly Meeting, if even insignificant he were to fail in
his duty. Besides he could do no good at home, so there
was no excuse for staying. The fact was he had had a
second lesson in the experiences of pioneers. This time it
was not money that Friends thought it right to withhold—it
was service. They really were very troublesome to the
authorities with their whims and scruples! There had been a
balloting for the militia, and Leonard, John's eldest brother,
had unfortunately been " drawn." He must serve himself,
find a substitute, or go to prison. His conscience would not
allow him to fight or to join in any preparation for fighting,
and it would be no better to send a substitute to do wrong
than to do wrong himself. The man who rented the shed in
the yard would gladly have taken Leonard's place for a
" consideration," or even if Leonard would do his work
when he was absent. He would like the change, and he
had taught Leonard to weave—there would be no difficulty
about that. But there were no crooked turns in Leonard's
conscience, and the idea could not be entertained for a
moment ; he must take the remaining alternative and go to
prison for a month. He had been in prison a fortnight
when John left home, and had another fortnight to remain.
The juvenile members of the family looked upon him as quite
a martyr, making a great demonstration when he returned ;
and even he seemed inclined to be "a bit set up," the neighbours said, because he had "suffered for conscience sake." It
was perhaps on this account that his mother strongly advised
him to read " Sewell's History of the Quakers," and learn

something of *real* suffering for conscience sake. Friends can scarcely desire the return of such treatment, but nothing would be more calculated to increase both the numbers and strength of the Society, terms which are by no means synonymous, though they seem to be often considered so.

John took up rather more room than on his last journey out of town, and, as he mounted to his seat behind the driver, felt altogether a different individual from the small member of the "cargo" which had travelled in a similar direction under female care. He was again going to new scenes and an untried life, but this time not entirely amongst strangers, and he felt no fear. His firm intention was to do his duty to his master's and mistress's satisfaction (such names were recognized then), and so to win their regard that—who could say what might happen? The future looked beautifully bright and simple, for he no longer remembered that long word, impracticability, standing at the head of his old spelling lesson. His dreams had so shortened the distance that he was astonished to find the coach pulling up at the Angel Inn, in Hallam, and rejoiced to see his friend Willie's cheery face waiting by the inn door to welcome him.

It was a long walk to Heatherby, but they had a great deal to say and would be glad of the time, so, leaving one box to follow, they took the smaller parcels and set off. The Hall, Willie said, as they tramped along, was partly built in Henry Eighth's time, and had been latterly inhabited by an old Judge. It was a curious, rambling place, but the Justice's room made a capital schoolroom, and the rest of the house proved equally serviceable. He had seen all the Doubledays; there were four sisters and three brothers; the baby, who used to watch them pass the cottage at Ackworth, was the youngest. Mr. Doubleday was as kind as ever, but his wife looked rather stern. He said nothing specially about Margaret, and John was not sorry.

We need not take up time with further introductions. Willie remarked on leaving, that he hoped to see John at meeting on " First-day," but he must be sure to be early if he wanted a seat. " It is not like our little lot of Friends at home."

CHAPTER VII.

Ministers.—A Convinced Friend.—Troubles.—John prefers Patience to Impracticability.

On arriving at the Meeting-house in good time, as was the habit of the family, John perceived the full force of Willie's parting remark. There was not a seat to spare, and a party of young people who came in ten minutes late could only be accommodated on a form placed in the middle aisle. There was a goodly array of " Friends in the gallery," too, which means Friends who, by the general consent of their monthly meeting, had been " recorded as ministers;" whose communications, whether of prayer or counsel, have been felt by the meeting to spring from the right source.

Friends believe that a heart in a state of silent, expectant waiting is often touched by Divine inspiration as directly and unmistakably as were the prophets of old. In our hurrying nineteenth-century lives it is more difficult, perhaps, to keep the quiet, concentrated frame of mind in which alone the still, small voice can be heard; but even yet amongst their ministers are many, women as well as men, ·

who speak with a power that their hearers feel is far beyond their natural one. No special instruction is thought necessary to prepare them—a message may be sent by the mouth of an unlettered minister as clearly as by the most learned, faith and obedience being equally possible to them both; but the mind that has been trained, whilst acquiring knowledge, to clear and orderly thought, certainly possesses an advantage over an untrained one; and the more cultured the individual —these essential elements of -faith and obedience being equal—the better can he or she appreciate and help the difficulties of those whose deeper insight into the laws and mysteries of the universe has brought them into much searching of heart.

The truth of Tennyson's words—" as the instrument, so comes the sound "—can scarcely be denied.

Hallam was particularly "favoured" in the way of ministers at that time, and amongst them was one who attracted John's notice at once from his open and benevolent countenance. Little but his countenance could be seen as he sat amongst his peers in the gallery; but after "meeting" John had the pleasure of being introduced to Daniel Brady, and found him to be of middle height, rather stout, but remarkably erect and square-shouldered, his hat, of much wider brim than any we see now, adding to his general appearance of breadth. He was then, and seemed always to be, dressed in a suit of dark coffee-coloured cloth.

He was what is called a "Convinced Friend," that is, he held his membership in the Society not by the plan peculiar to it, of "birthright membership," but by voluntarily applying for admission because the Quaker views and principles were the nearest he could find to his ideal of truth. Convinced Friends are, as a rule, stricter and more earnest than the born members, who too often have accepted their position and opinions without examining them. Daniel Brady was one of the most earnest and gifted. His life had been a rugged one until the age of twenty-five. Part of the time engaged in the navy, the last four years in the army, he had experienced, to the full extent, the hardships inseparable from both situations, and he had not escaped their temptations, nor passed scatheless through them.. When nearly twenty-five years old his regiment was ordered to the West Indies, under Sir Ralph Abercrombie, and it was during the voyage out, in the midst of a severe storm, that his conscience was finally awakened to the consequences of his unsteady life.

He took counsel of no one. He afterwards said of himself, "No human means were made use of—it was altogether the immediate work of the Holy Spirit on my heart." Submitting to the guidance and discipline of that Spirit, he soon felt his profession to be out of keeping with the commands, "Love your enemies," and "Do good to them that hate you," which are the burden of the New Testament. On his return to England he gave up his commission in the army, and betook himself to Hallam, where his eldest sister had married a "Quaker." Finding, as we said before, that their views were nearer to his ideal than any he had met with, he sought admission to the Society, and followed his sister's example by marrying one of its members. He became a partner in an ale and porter business in Hallam, and also opened a shop in the seed trade. But remarkable as his life was, it only claims a corner in our simple annals because of its intimate connection in after years with that of one of our young friends. His eldest son was already under Wm. Doubleday's care, Daniel Brady told John, and the other three would follow, he hoped, as they grew old enough. Two or three friends had guaranteed Wm. Doubleday £200 a-year if he would open this school at Hallam, but it increased so rapidly they were not called upon for the money. As usual, his pupils idolized him, one of them says.

We will not go into the details of school life again, but will content ourselves with the general announcement that it was like life everywhere, made up of small things, some sweet, some bitter. The pleasant things predominated in John's lot at first. He made the personal acquaintance of Margaret and her brothers and sisters, and found them, on the whole, pleasant young people. They were strikingly various, both in appearance and character. Elizabeth, the next to Margaret, was the literary lady of the family, and contrived to leave her share of household duties to the others to do for her if they were willing, or to be left undone if they were not, while she slipped away to her books. Sarah, her younger sister, was full of kindness and comicality, but she was decidedly of the opinion that people ought to attend to their own business, and occasionally refused to screen her sister; and then, for a time, there was trouble amongst them, but not for long. Mary, the youngest, was at school at Ackworth, and so was the second brother. Wm. Doubleday's eldest son assisted him in the school, and the youngest, the baby of Ackworth memory, was now an independent young man of five years old. They were all thrown constantly together, for it was a busy household. Mrs. Doubleday was an active woman, and she took care that everyone was well employed about her. Her daughters and servants were kept fully occupied and even the two apprentices were asked for help sometimes, a request that would excite neither surprise nor displeasure in those days.

John certainly had no objection to sit under the large sycamores at the edge of the back lawn helping to shell peas, or to bring his copy-book stitching into the dining-room when the girls were engaged in folding clothes or repairing the linen before they laid it by. Willie often joined them in the evening, the second apprentice was full of fun, and they were a lively company. Repeating poetry was a great resource; they either took turns in reciting long pieces and extracts, or they cut them up into disjointed fragments by the game of "Capping Verses." Willie used to repeat canto after canto from Byron with all the greater gusto because it was only half approved; John preferred Cowper's Fireside; Elizabeth gave them extempore morsels if she was at a loss for a verse beginning with the right letter; and Alfred, John's comrade, made puns upon everything, and looked all the while as sober as the old judge himself used to look when he sat in the opposite room.

The renewal of his old companionship with Willie was another of John's pleasant things; they spent as much time together as possible. As the older established man of business, Willie was full of importance and good advice, and often instruction too, for it was one of John's sage rules for self-discipline to lose no opportunity of adding to his knowledge. Whether in his own line or not did not signify, knowledge of any kind was sure to be useful some time; therefore, by permission of the two masters, Willie passed on to him the lessons in map and plan-drawing he received in the office, or in the practical work of surveying, whenever there was an afternoon to spare, receiving, in return, literary instruction of one kind or another. It was good for them both.

John learned book-binding for the benefit of the school. A small square barn or granary stood on one side of the house, and its upper story was used for a workshop; the book-binder's press was there, and most of the stationery used by the boys was prepared in that little room. Gardening was a favourite occupation with all of them. In the large grounds, that had become picturesque in their wildness during the Justice's lifetime, there was abundant scope for talent of various kinds. One part was allotted to the pupils, and each of the family had a separate garden of his or her own. It was a peaceful and happy life, full of work and full of interest.

The first little break in the harmony of it was the intro- duction amongst them of two young Africans, known as Sandanec and Mahmadec. African affairs were receiving a large share of attention just then,—the great anti-slavery movement had begun,—and many plans for helping and improving the negroes were proposed and tried by the "Friends of African Civilization," as they were called at first. Sierra Leone they hoped to make a centre from which instruction would spread for the enlightenment of the whole continent. To prepare native teachers for schools there, was of course one of the first steps, and amongst the captured slaves who were brought to London, any who seemed parti- cularly intelligent, were detained, if possible, to be educated for that purpose. By some means, Wm. Doubleday had been prevailed upon to undertake these two. Mahmadee was a Jaloof prince, but what Sandanee's former life had been was very uncertain. The Doubledays imagined it must have been something wild, judging by the strange impulses that seized him at times and the impossibility of teaching him "manners." Mahmadee was a gentle, thoughtful boy, and returned to useful life in his own country; so far as is known, Sandanee never went back, but he was unfortunately lost sight of when he grew up. They were not always an agreeable addition to the family.

The second interruption to the home life at Heatherby was the illness of Mrs. Doubleday. She was for a long time unable to take her place in the household, and her duties fell upon Margaret, which was a heavy charge for a girl of sixteen. The young housekeeper had grown to her full height by that time, and with her hair smoothened under a cap, as custom then demanded, she looked considerably older than she really was, which she found a great advantage. John had never wavered in his secret determination, and now more than ever he admired the clever dignified girl, but he wisely restricted himself for a long time to expressing his feelings by quietly watching for opportunities to help her; attending to the little brother, and taking care amongst other things that her garden did not suffer for her close confinement in the house. It is not to be supposed that Margaret was blind to these attentions; certainly those around her were not, excepting perhaps the two individuals whose favour was most important. The young people were out of the range of the mother's observant sight, and the father's vision was not keen; but he would not have disapproved if he had been conscious of their feelings.

As was incidentally mentioned in a former chapter, William Doubleday, like Daniel Brady, was a "convinced Friend;" but he was one of quite a different type from the ex-soldier. He lacked the training and discipline that the latter had undergone, and his naturally impressionable and sympathetic disposition would have been strengthened by such an influence; so it seems to us, at least, with our limited horizon. Yet who shall say that the extreme views of direct inspiration which took possession of him in later years were wrong for him, or that, because they led him away from the outwardly successful life that seemed now opening before him, he was entirely mistaken in following them. "Success in life" may have a different meaning for us a century hence. Soon after his marriage he had been disinherited by his father for leaving the Established Church, of which all his family were members, and joining the Methodists; that the greater quietness of the Friends afterwards induced him to make another change was, if anything, a further offence. Whatever seemed to him right, he would do without considering consequences; he would have walked to the stake, if duty pointed to it, with a firm step and a beaming face. Such was Margaret's father. One little plan of his for managing his own young children may, perhaps, be alluded to here. We said, only a few lines further back, that his vision was not keen, which was quite true in reference to such matters as we were then speaking of; but for selfishness, unkindness, or anything approaching to a quarrel, his eyes and ears were painfully open. He did not, however, always deem it wise to speak at the moment; it might even be a day or two afterwards that the little offender would find in drawer or desk, a single verse or a simple narrative in rhyme that would recall to mind some exhibition of temper or act of selfishness that deserved reproof.

> "Said the flint to the steel, if you'd not so much fire,
> You'd be just such a steel as a flint might desire ;
> Said the steel to the flint, when you let me alone
> I'm as cool as yourself, so the fault is your own,"

was quite understood by the little tease who had roused a sister's anger.

"Alick, 1 have to finish some ciphering-books this evening ; if thou would like to fetch thy rocking-chair I will carry it up to the workshop for thee, and thou can watch me 'plough,' as thou calls it," said John to his little favourite one evening after tea, and the invitation was gladly accepted. Alick liked the workshop, there was always something interesting going on in it, and from its two windows he could keep a lookout upon the movements about the house, for one window commanded the front door, and the other the gardens and far-stretching fields. He was necessarily very much left to himself, and his chief enjoyment was to sit in his little rocking-chair swinging backwards and forwards in the "Apple-for-a-King and Pear-for-a-Queen" style, shouting his favourite verses or chanting them melodiously to a "tune of his own composing." So the rocking-chair was invited as well as Alick.

> "Her firefly lamp I soon shall see,
> Her paddle I soon shall hear,"

the little fellow was beginning as usual—for the Dismal Swamp was his special piece, and that verse of it a particular favourite—when he suddenly started up with the exclamation, "Why! there's mother! she is coming out for a walk. Father is bringing her!"

John went to the window; it really was Mrs. Doubleday. He had heard from day to day lately that she was improving, but he was taken by surprise to see her out. She was leaning upon her husband's arm; he and the bright warm evening had lured her to make the attempt. She looked up at the workshop window, and gave the apprentice a smile, the last she gave him for a long time. Alick had already deserted him, and rushed downstairs to join them in their walk. They wandered slowly on towards the gardens; how beautiful everything appeared to the invalid after being so long a prisoner!

"Look, Mother! this is my garden; is not my pond pretty? Sister let me have the bowl," said the happy little boy.

"Very pretty, dear; but this is the prettiest and best kept of the whole. Which of you does that belong to?"

"Oh! that is Margaret's; isn't it beautiful?"

"Margaret's! but Margaret has no time for gardening, I am sure! How is that?"

"Oh! John Skelton does it for her; he is *so* kind."

Mrs. Doubleday gave an involuntary glance, not this time a smiling one, at the old granary window, which John happened to see, and a strange foreboding came over him. His old spelling lesson returned to his mind, and the seven-syllabled word that he so strongly objected to seemed determined to find a place for itself in his dictionary. Im-prac-ti-ca-bil-i-ty he spelled once again, with his hands mentally behind his back. But there was another word that he liked much better, a shorter one, and that was—Patience, and he finally determined to have faith in it still.

"I am afraid, my dear," said Mrs. Doubleday to her

husband on their return to the house, "that I have been needed downstairs more than thou imagines. What does this mean about the gardens?"

"Is there any hidden meaning in it, my dear Sarah? I do not understand."

She quickly made him understand her view of it; but met with little sympathy in her objections. What did the different social positions of their families signify if the young man's character was satisfactory? He must make a position for himself; and that, if his master was not mistaken, he was very likely to do: *his* only objection, supposing his wife's suspicions to be correct, was their youth—they did not know their own minds.

She could find nothing to say against John's character, and neither he nor Margaret could be sent away, they were too useful at home, besides there was no real ground for speaking; it might be only Mrs. Doubleday's idea, which it would be foolish to suggest needlessly.

And so it rested; there was no immediate explanation, but an indefinably uncomfortable feeling crept amongst them, as if they were walking at the edge of a precipice.

Just as peace was settling over Europe, discord was finding its way to secluded Heatherby.

CHAPTER VIII.

The Emperor Alexander of Russia.—Daniel Brady.—Okta.

The temporary peace, as it proved, of 1814 brought the Allied Powers, with Alexander I. of Russia at their head, to sojourn for a time in Paris. At the invitation of our Prince

Regent, Alexander crossed the Channel to England, accompanied by his sister, the Duchess of Oldenburg. His antecedents, so far as we know them, would not be of much advantage even to our friend the professor in the study of his character, I am afraid; for, to use the professor's own words, "the initial influence of his life seems to lie too far in the past for human mind to trace." We can scarcely imagine him to be indebted to his immediate ancestors for his just, humane, and unselfish character. His inclinations and his circumstances seemed constantly at variance. Theoretically his sympathies had always been with France, the France of the republic, notwithstanding his own position as despotic ruler of between sixty and seventy millions of people; and his feeling towards England was not especially cordial when he first set foot on English soil. But he found a great deal going on here that interested and delighted him, though much also that he did not approve. For one thing, he very strongly objected to the long sitting after dinner, which was then carried to an extreme ; he would rather have been learning something about the objects that were constantly in his mind whenever he could free it from the affairs of the camp. The younger and less important members of the Royal family were more congenial companions to him than the "first gentleman of Europe"—their tastes were more alike. Education and agriculture possessed the greatest interest for him, and in the former of these the Dukes of Kent and Sussex were thoroughly interested too. A variety of philanthropic work was going on—slavery and capital punishment were being valiantly fought, and men of various religious opinions and stations in life worked in harmony for these ends who would else, probably, never have known of each other's existence. As might be expected, many of the Society of Friends came well to the front, and their judicious and intelligent labours brought them prominently into notice. In this way the Emperor became acquainted with several of them, and they seemed to him a people eminently to possess the qualities that he would gladly cultivate in his own dominions, to the displacing, if possible, the insincerity, love of display, and many undesirable habits that he was painfully conscious were the characteristics of his own subjects; and he took every opportunity of informing himself as to Quaker opinions and practice.

He attended one of their meetings at Westminster, and by special desire had private conversations with some of them afterwards, making minute inquiries as to their lives and the manner in which they carried out the principles that had so pleased him in theory. He was surprised to find that oaths and tests still kept them from a share in the government and in the advantages of university education, and he could perhaps scarcely realise the different spirit of the two countries in dealing with obstructions. If *he* saw that a thing wanted altering he had only to publish a ukase, and the change was made at once, on the surface at least; and the slower, if safer, manner of legislating in England was a new experience to him.

Alexander expressed a wish to see a Friend's house, and an arrangement was made for him to call at one in Brighton, on his way back to town from Portsmouth; but the crowd was so great he could not stop, and no further opportunity seemed to present itself. He made one for himself, however. As he and his party were on their journey to Dover when they returned to the Continent, they noticed two Friends standing at the door of a house at a little distance from the road. The Emperor stopped his carriage, got out, and courteously inquired of them if they belonged to the people commonly called Quakers. On receiving a reply in the affirmative he next asked leave for himself and sister to enter the house, which of course was granted. They stayed some time, looking over it, taking refreshment, and telling their host and hostess, to whom it was news, of their attending a meeting, and their interviews with members of the Society, in London. Here his favourable opinion of Friends was confirmed—the farm and the house were well cared for and orderly; and he did not forget his impressions when the time came for making use of them.

Three years afterwards, when, having a little leisure for attending to the affairs most pleasing to him, he decided on draining and cultivating the marsh lands round St. Petersburg, he remembered his visit to England and his favourable ideas of English agriculture, and he directed that enquiry should be made for an Englishman to come out and superintend the work, particularly requesting that he should be a member of the Society of Friends.

Where was such a man to be found? He would need much more than a knowledge of agriculture; he must have the power to control others as well as to arrange their work; he must be able to stand before princes with propriety and dignity, and withal he must be one who would uphold the credit and honour not only of the Society which had so attracted the Emperor but of their and his great Master. Information of his wish was spread amongst their different meetings, and it seemed especially to find rest in Hallam. Our friend Daniel Brady might have been—no doubt had been—pre-

7

paring for this post. His mind for the last two years had been turned in the direction of foreign service of some kind, and when this invitation was made known he felt it was sent to him. As if to complete his fitness for the work, he had taken a farm a short distance from the town, and for two or three years had been practising agriculture with the greatest success, developing a latent·talent for it that surprised everybody. Therefore when the enquiry reached Hallam the manager was ready. To his surprise and unbounded relief, his wife was also ready; Ruth's language to Naomi rose to her lips, and she encouraged him to make any sacrifice for the sake of duty.

He offered himself and was gladly accepted, the Emperor showing his implicit confidence by sending to him an agreement or bond, already bearing the Imperial signature, but with the *amount* of salary a blank for Daniel Brady to fill up according to his own choice. We are sure the confidence was not misplaced. He went over to St. Petersburg the same year to have an interview with Alexander, and to make arrangements for going out with his family the following summer. From the oldest to the youngest, all were to accompany him. The Emperor had asked his intentions as to that, and rejoiced when he heard what they were : it was not only farming he wanted, he said—it was their good influence quite as much.

John wrote to his brother Harry at this time, " We took tea at Daniel Brady's last evening ; that is the Friend who is going out to Russia next summer with all his family. He is there now to see the ground and plans." John's own future had not yet shown itself. Many details wanted considering on Daniel Brady's return. Two of his sons were now at Wm. Doubleday's school; the oldest had left and would be able to help his father; but besides these there were a fourth son and two daughters whose education must be continued by some means. He felt he could not do better than consult his friend at Heatherby, so he walked up there one fine evening and laid his wants before him. Wm. Doubleday was of all others the man to enter into his feelings, and as it proved, to help him out of his difficulties.

"Thou must take a teacher with thee, Daniel; there is no question as to that."

"Just so; that seems the only plan for securing that the children shall not suffer; but where shall I find him? We shall have difficulties to contend with, and we shall be like a city set on a hill; and, besides these considerations, the man I want should be able to do something more than give book lessons—he must know how to use his hands, and such a man is not met with every day. However, I cannot lose faith that I shall be helped in *all* things, the path has been made so clear before me thus far."

"The man is waiting for thee, I think, Daniel, as thou wast waiting for the Emperor, and the move will be a mutual advantage; indeed, I may say an advantage to all of us. Thou hast frequently met with my apprentice, John Skelton?"

"Yes; but he is very young."

"He is very steady, and, I think, combines all the qualities thou art looking for. As to himself, it will be of untold good to him to be under thy care. If the idea commends itself to thy mind, I will give him the remainder of his apprenticeship, partly for his and thy advantage, and partly to get him out of my house!"

The last few words of this speech, if uttered by some
people, would have thrown a doubt on the purity of motive
in recommending John, but not when they came from Wm.
Doubleday. They only required an explanation, which was
given to his visitor's entire satisfaction. My readers will
need no help in supplying it for themselves. The details of
arrangement may also be left to the same intelligence, as
well as John Skelton's mixed feelings of gratitude and
pleasure, and of regret at leaving the place which had been
to him so happy a home.

Something of an understanding was allowed about, but
not with, Margaret. Neither engagement nor correspondence
was permitted, and the mother's objections were unshaken;
but John felt that Wm. Doubleday was his ally, and again
he said to himself—Patience !

There was busy work at the Skelton's. The honour it
was to their "boy" to be thus chosen, his wonderful
ambition and perseverance, his mother and sister were never
tired of talking about, as they prepared to "set him off"
for the third time in his life. They understood now his
preference for the boarding-school, yet were very doubtful
as to the fulfilling of his wishes. But, in any case, "John
would do his duty; " and to " go abroad," under the care of
such a man as Daniel Brady, was in itself a privilege. To
" go abroad" at all was a privilege out of the reach of many
people in 1818.

The party we know, with the addition of two labourers
and their families, set sail from Hull in the Arethusa, on the
22nd of June in that year, under the command of pleasant
and genial Captain Wharton, and on July 8th, John says, in
his first letter home, " the guard-ship's boat boarded us, and

we had our first near view of the Russians." The evening before they had been close enough to Cronstadt to hear the Admiral's sunset gun. It had been a quick passage of only sixteen days. The Arethusa could go no further than Cronstadt; the depth of water in the Neva was variable, and often insufficient, and the transit of goods from this port to the city frequently took as long as the rest of the voyage. However, our travellers had good accommodation on board, and remained in their own quarters. There was no need for haste.

The King of Prussia was visiting the Emperor, and the capital was given up to military display and festivity; the English farmers must wait. But in the midst of his regal hospitality Alexander had not forgotten his *protegés*. A house belonging to Count Bezborodka, near the village of Okta, a mile and a half outside the city gates, was placed at their disposal, with orders that everything Daniel Brady required from the vessel was to be landed duty-free, and what was deficient in the house was to be supplied according to his wishes. The kind consideration of their Imperial master never failed them during their stay in his empire. At length our party were ready to leave the vessel, and were transferred to a large boat with twelve oars, for the passage to the city. They hoped to reach Okta the same evening, but the current of the Neva was against them, they were nine hours on the water, and did not land until eleven o'clock, too late to continue their journey that night. They therefore sent on the two men, with their families and goods, by the lighter to Okta, and themselves stayed at an inn. The next morning John and Daniel Brady's eldest son wandered into the city to look about them, and were wonder-

ing if they liked the uniform rows of delicately-tinted stuc-
coed houses, when they were suddenly apprised by two officers
riding rapidly down the street that the Emperor was coming,
and everyone uncovered. Here was a trial for them at once;
but they did what they believed to be right, and kept on
their hats. He was shortsighted, but the fact of theirs being
the only two heads covered as he passed led him to observe
them attentively, and he probably came to the right con-
clusion as to their identity, for he had noticed in England
this departure from the usual custom, and had been informed
of Friends' reason for it—that they considered it a mark of
homage which ought to be paid only to the Almighty. As
the Emperor did not object, no notice was taken of it.

In the afternoon they drove to their new home, and found
it an excellent house containing twenty-four rooms. The
two men and their families were accommodated in the lower
part, and the kitchens were also on the ground floor; a room
was set aside there for "meeting," and Daniel Brady and
his family, according to the custom of the country, occupied
the upper twelve. There was a high wall round the yard to
keep out the wolves at night. The Neva at this point was
about half a mile broad, and the house was pleasantly situated
on its bank. They were kept lively, John says, in that same
letter, "by the incredible number of barks or rafts which
float past to the city every day, laden with hemp, tallow,
and provisions from noblemen's estates in the interior, and
brought down by the current of the river. They are con-
structed of deal, and on disposing of the cargo the men who
bring them sell the barks for firewood or other purposes, and
return with the proceeds on foot to their owners, of whom
men as well as barks are the absolute property."

Beds and necessary furniture of that kind had been provided for the family, which was fortunate, as they arrived before the lighter, and when the boat came the next day all hands were ready to unload and put in order the household goods they had brought from England. Amongst them was a fine old-fashioned eight-day clock, which was set up in a corner of the common sitting-room. They thought it would be particularly useful to have a trustworthy timepiece for general reference, but a use was made of it that never entered into their calculations.

In every Russian dwelling, the poorest as well as the most sumptuous, there may be seen in a corner of the entrance, or of the "living-room," generally facing you as you go in, a sort of square metal picture representing a saint or some occurrence in the life of one, often by figures that seem to us very grotesque. These images vary in size, material, and finish; the cheapest are not more than an inch or two square, the more costly reaching the size of one or two feet. All orthodox members of the Greek church on entering the room bow towards the image and cross themselves before speaking to the master or mistress of the house. On looking round for the usual object of momentary worship in Daniel Brady's room, his visitors could find nothing so nearly resembling it as the eight-day clock, and without noticing the protest of its owner they continued so to regard it.

Two or three weeks elapsed, and each day household affairs became more settled; Russian stoves and other conveniences were better understood and more highly appreciated, and our friends felt themselves at liberty to begin their special work out of doors. They were indeed very anxious to begin it, for the summer was rapidly running its course; they were near the end of July, and in October possibly, though not certainly, they might be suddenly driven from the land by the hardening frost. They had, of course, examined the piece they were to commence upon on this side of the city; it was a plot of about a thousand acres, as far from their residence as that was from the city gates. It proved not so boggy as John expected; it was rather spongey than boggy, being covered with white moss, on an average sixteen inches deep, with cowberry and other pretty bog plants, and young fir trees, not tall, but seriously interfering with their lines in surveying.

An interpreter had been sent to reside with them, as they decided to leave the study of the language for the short dark days of winter. Lessons of all kinds, indeed, were deferred until then, for out-door work pressed upon them, and the tutor was promptly called upon for some of the hand-work that Daniel Brady had foreseen might be wanted from him. A Russian surveyor had been promised for their assistance, and he came, but when he was directed to take a level, he was obliged to confess his ignorance—he had never done such a thing! So John's Hallam lessons proved useful, and confirmed him in his appreciation of that sage rule of which we have already spoken, "Lose no opportunity of gaining knowledge." Daniel Brady's eldest son William and he set to work and did their best, and John used to say one of the "proudest moments of his life" was when, at the end of the summer, they saw the water run successfully down the drains in this first plot at Okta.

But this is looking too far in advance: they were only planning their work yet. They proposed to carry all round the boundary a wide deep drain that would have a good fall into the river Okta, and that would serve for a fence as well as a general outlet. Wolves must be taken into consideration in preparing for the future, that pleasant future when they hoped to see these acres dotted with dwellings amongst verdant pastures and fields of waving corn! They would next intersect their plot with smaller drains, cutting it up into fields of about eight acres each, small fields, but their land was almost level and the drains must be close accordingly. As soon as the surface was sufficiently dry they would proceed to hack up the moss. In experimenting a little upon this, they discovered that beneath the foot and half of sphagnum there were the roots of an old forest, and occasionally, near the surface, some large tree trunks in an advanced stage of decay, which would effectually prevent the use of a plough, and compel them to break up the surface by hand labour.

There would be no difficulty about this, however, as there might have been at home; the Emperor would supply them with everything they required, men included. They had already been promised three hundred "soldiers" for the work, and began to wish they would make their appearance; the few men already here could only just help them in their experiments. For some things it was pleasant to farm on this ask-and-have system, with no anxiety as to whether it would pay, but to men whose honest desire was to *make* it pay and to get their work done, the dilatory style of transacting business around them was very painful. They all had need of John's favourite—because, he felt, for himself so much needed—word, Patience. "In Russia," as Mr. Wallace says, "time is *not* money." In the course of their poking about, they found amongst the roots part of a bombshell and a Swedish axe, which led them to suppose the forest might have been destroyed in the wars between Charles XII. of Sweden and Peter the Great; they had previously concluded that it had been felled to furnish timber for the building of the city; the "window" Peter wisely felt was wanted "to look out of into Europe."

The long wished for soldiers came at last; explicit instructions had been received as to the preparations to be made for them or Daniel Brady would have been at a loss, and would certainly not have provided what seemed to be expected. He was ordered to prepare long shelves, six feet wide, against the wall of a wooden building, to serve as beds; here they slept, in their clothes, side by side, apparently comfortable or at least apathetic; their dining table was a plank and tressels—the black bread and onions of their usual mid-day meal needed no dishes. Indeed it seemed at first sight that they might have called a table a luxury and dispensed with it altogether, but it proved useful for holding, at intervals of a few feet, the little heaps . of salt that they shook out of a curious bottle-like receptable made of the inner bark of the birch. And that was all. They were to be paid thirty kopeks, or about threepence a day, in money, clothes and food being also found by the Emperor. William Brady and John were ready with their plans and at five o'clock next morning arranged their men, each armed with a spade, at equal distances on the line of the proposed boundary drain. They were expecting them to begin when they were startled and impressed by the preliminary movement; as by one impulse these peasants, dirty, bearded, and loosely garmented, removed their caps, crossed themselves devoutly, and prayed in a few words to the Virgin Mary to intercede for a blessing on the work begun that day. The same desire, with variations, had been in their own hearts and notwithstanding the errors and superstition they could not help feeling a sympathy with these Russian boors, whose language they could not yet understand. But I am afraid there was not much ground for real sympathy. A recent writer says: "In all that regards externals" the Russian peasant "is decidedly religious"; and that is exactly what can be said of it. His religion is external only, and does not touch the spring of his actions. John used to say "he would cross himself with one hand and rob you with the other," religion and conduct had nothing to do with each other, according to Russian ideas, and, perhaps, we could find the same division nearer home, too.

By slow degrees the drains were cut, and the moss gathered off the land, and the next operation was the stubbing up of the tree roots, and the laying them in a line down the middle of each field to dry, and become lighter before their removal the following spring. The moss was also left in heaps for the winter; some powder magazines were situated not far away, and it was forbidden to burn the rubbish on the land. By very slow degrees it was that the work proceeded; English energy was disgusted and despairing. "The Russian peasant," says Mr. Wallace, "has a capacity of patient endurance that would do honour to a martyr, and a power of continued dogged passive resistance such as is possessed I believe by no other class of men in Europe, and these qualities form a very powerful barrier against the rapacity of unconscientious proprietors." This so exactly expresses the character given of them by our friends sixty years ago that it is interesting

to find it also the opinion of a traveller who has been amongst
them so lately. The qualities he speaks of were no doubt
useful to the poor serfs as a defence from the rapacity of
their owners; but they also formed a barrier against the
honest desire of conscientious employers to finish their work
in proper time.

After long consideration Daniel Brady decided to try
another plan with the men; he had tried appealing to their
sense of duty, he would now appeal to their self-interest.
He had them assembled, and told them through the interpreter that "their father the Emperor" had ordered him to
give them threepence a day, and he had obeyed his orders.
But that in the country he came from people only expected
three-penny-worth of work for threepence; and he proposed
to measure off a certain quantity of work that he considered
worth the money, and when they had done it they might go
for the day; or, if they wished to earn a little more, whatever
they did after that should be measured at night and paid for
at the same rate. The men were astonished at the address,
but the work went on more briskly next morning when the
plan was tried. The greater number left, however, when
the allotted piece was done; some because they were too
idle to work, others because they did not believe the promises.
A few continued to dig, and at night their work was carefully measured and of course paid for to the full. As they
went away delighted with their extra gains and surveying
the money actually in their hands, they remarked with
surprise one to another, " Why, this man does as he says he
will!" an instructive comment on the usual style of treating
them. The plan was kept up, and had a marked effect upon
the work, but this small experience gave them an idea of the

manner in which the ruler of such a people could be quietly
and passively thwarted in his best endeavours for the general
good.

Much curiosity was excited about this scheme of the
Emperor's, and the strange people that he had brought into
the country, but his favour secured them from annoyance,
and very soon they were better known and appreciated.
They had many visitors, and amongst them were many from
the court. As Wm. Brady and John were surveying on the
land near the road, one day, a carriage stopped, and the
Minister of the Interior descended and approached them;
their hands were in a condition that may be imagined, from
dragging the chain and clearing away obstructions, and in
any case they would not have *offered* to shake hands, but he
insisted on it with great warmth and cordiality. The
Empress came more than once to call upon them, delighting
them by her simple and unassuming manners; and another
day they received a message that they might expect the
Emperor that afternoon, but that no special preparation was
to be made for him. He enjoyed escaping from the pomp
and ceremony of the court, and walking or driving about the
city unattended; he arrived at Okta accompanied only by the
coachman who had been with him in England. He made
Daniel Brady take the second seat in his Droschky, and show
him everything they had done and were doing, telling him,
after a tour of inspection that had lasted a couple of hours,
" You have done a great deal of work since you came, Mr.
Brady." On returning to the house, their august visitor
joined the family at tea, and told them he should like to
come again. There was a little check on free conversation,
because Daniel Brady did not speak French, and the

Emperor's English was not thoroughly fluent; if they could have expressed themselves to each other more easily, he said to "Allen and Grellett," as he used to call them, he should go to Okta more frequently. One ear was deaf, too, which increased the difficulty; but both he and the Empress objected to the presence of an interpreter during these visits—they preferred to manage as well as they could without him. The Emperor had shown, on his return from England, that he felt a knowledge of our language to be desirable, by ordering that it should be taught in all schools throughout the Empire.

John sent home an account of this visit, which gratified everybody very much. I dare say his letters were great treasures, and that his father felt very proud to be able to give news of "my son, who is with Daniel Brady in St. Petersburg." He had also written to his old master soon after landing, hoping to be allowed to keep up a correspondence with him, but it was flagging, and at present his only medium of communication with Hallam and Heatherby was his old friend Willie Dunning.

Fortunately for our agriculturists, winter delayed its approach this year. "It was not until November 11 "— John mentions the date particularly, perhaps remembering as he wrote that it was Margaret's birthday—"that a strong westerly wind broke up the ice in Lake Ladoga, which came floating down for fifteen days afterwards." Then followed the real Russian winter; the broken flakes and lumps of ice froze together again in the Neva, and roads were levelled across it, marked out by fir trees, where the floating bridges had been. This weather would last for six months, and arrangements were made in good earnest accordingly; amongst other preparations, the second windows were put up, and a thermometer was hung outside, in such a position that it could be seen from the room and consulted before leaving the house, as a guide to the amount of clothing to put on; the cold was so intense it was not safe to risk stepping out to try. And yet it was not a severe winter, they were told, which was considered a calamity; there was not so much sledging in consequence, and sledging was a delightful means of locomotion at the beginning of the season at least. The gliding along during the first few weeks while the snow was smooth and hard, or during the whole winter in the unfrequented parts, was like that "of a boat in calm water;" but when the ice and snow had been cut up by much travelling it was more like the same boat on a billowy sea. One winter while they were there the deeply snow-covered road between St. Petersburg and Moscow was worn so full of holes by the sledges that many people were thoroughly *sea-sick* on the journey.

Sledges were very handsome looking conveyances; their strong frame-work was only rough, but when a richly-coloured carpet was thrown over the back, and plenty of furs about the feet and knees, the general appearance was truly luxurious. They were, like the carriages in summer, drawn by three horses abreast; or, to speak correctly, they were *drawn* by one horse trotting in the shafts, accompanied by two outsiders, whose business it was to gallop gracefully, one on his left, the other on his right, at the same time bending their heads away from him with a peculiar turn, which had a very showy effect. This is not, as a recent writer has allowed his imagination to explain, the consequence of the animals' desire to watch the whip-hand of their driver, but is the result of deliberate training, and each side horse can only run on the side he is trained for. The head of the middle one is held high by a bearing-rein carried over a lofty arched collar; all three have long glossy tails, and being affectionately cared for, their appearance is splendid. It is a plan, fortunately for their horses, that could only be adopted in a country where horses are plentiful and space ample, but it seems to be still kept up in the Imperial city of the north.

"We watched an amusing scene to-day from our windows," John writes to his friend at Hallam. "A large handsome sledge, full of richly-dressed gentlemen and ladies, was upset just opposite the house. People are often toppled over. We knew there was no danger and no chance of their being hurt, so we could join in their hearty laughter as they rolled over and over in the snow. Their beautiful fur-lined silks were so slippery, it was impossible to rise, and they could neither help each other nor find a resting-place for arm or foot by which to raise themselves. Of course, we did not only laugh; as soon as we could get into our own furs we went to their help."

Frosted provisions do not keep in a mild winter, which is another calamity; and the ice to supply the ice-houses for the following summer is not so thick and firm as is desired. There would be more danger of finding that the cream had slipped on to the floor, because the blocks of ice—many of them three feet square—had begun to melt, and that is disappointing. The ice-houses were double buildings, the internal one, its floor covered with these blocks, having a passage round it after the fashion of the British Museum reading room. The servant shut the outer door before opening that of the inner apartment, which was visited many times a day in summer. It was not merely a storehouse of ice as a luxury for the table, but was the common larder for provisions. Boards were laid across the immense blocks to hold the food, but even then it was often impossible to keep it from one day to another in the hot season. The frosted provisions spoken of refer to a custom of freezing carcases whole, instead of salting them to preserve them for use. What is called "the frozen market" was held three days before Christmas, and must have been a curious sight; all sorts of animals, killed and frozen, were to be bought there, and the custom was for a housekeeper to purchase two or three, or more, according to the size of the family, keep them whole in his ice-cellar, and in an evening chop off with an axe the joint required for the next day's dinner and lay it on the stove all night to thaw. The axe was needed for the flesh as well as the bone, they being equally hard and splintery. The flavour was not quite so good as that of fresh meat, but the plan was a great convenience.

These new scenes and new experiences seemed to shorten the winter; our friends were surprised that they did not feel it irksome. John was required to spend four hours each day with the children at lessons, and the rest of the time was his own, which he thought a grand opportunity for study. The worst was the scarcity of letters; the frost stopped the communication with England by water, and though Count Lieven, the Russian Ambassador in London, had orders to forward with his own, all letters sent to him for the Emperor's "good friends the Quakers," there was probably a shyness amongst the correspondents at home about

8

availing themselves of this channel. The health of the whole party was remarkably good, but much as they enjoyed the winter altogether, they were not sorry when "the ice left them."

CHAPTER IX.

Volkova.—Almost Desponding.—Return to England.

The little plot of a thousand acres at Okta was nearly all cleared, and part of it rapidly greening over with its first crop of grass, when John was sent to the Volkova district, on the south side of the city, about five versts (three miles) on the Moscow road. Here there was a tract of 50,000 acres for them to bring into cultivation, and he was to commence operations on a portion of it. He had a couple of hundred men under his command, whose labours in clearing and draining the ground it was his duty to superintend. They were eight miles from the establishment at Okta, too far to go and come each day, as they began work at five o'clock in the morning; the village of Volkova was about equally distant in another direction, and, of course, equally inconvenient. The only other dwelling was a small wooden house inhabited by an old Russian peasant, who lived quite alone and did everything for himself; a venerable-looking old man, whose white beard and simple dress gave him a patriarchal, almost a hermit-like, appearance. Here John could be accommodated with a lodging, and be saved a great deal of fatigue if he would manage to cook for himself. Under the circumstances he was not only willing, but he preferred to try rather than run the risk of what he might other-

wise be called upon to eat. Cookery had not been one of the
accomplishments taught at Ackworth, but the domestic
knowledge of various kinds that the boys could not help
picking up there, added to a little common sense, enabled
him to get along quite easily. Daniel Brady came twice
a-week to see him, and bring "provisions to the garrison,"
as he said ; and John returned to Okta on a Saturday evening, to spend Sunday there, and join his friends in the little
meeting, which they regularly kept up. "It is noon here
two hours before it is with you," he said, in one of his letters
to his father ; "and when we are concluding our little meeting I often think you are just walking up Kilvert-street to
join yours."

It was a lonely life for him at Volkova, but the months in
which they could work on the land being only from May
until the breaking up of the ice in Lake Ladoga (which was
an uncertain date), he managed very well, and looked forward to the winter season for a return of rest and sociability.
He rose at four, made his bed, swept his room with a bundle
of birch twigs, prepared breakfast, and left all as tidy and
bright as if he daily expected a visit from the Emperor.
External dirt and disorder, he used to say, tended to a disorderly state of mind. But though contented with what
seemed best for the time, it was an intense pleasure to him to
have the weekly refreshment of English conversation with
his friends at Okta. His twenty-first birthday came whilst
he was alone in his wooden " box," for the old man and he
exchanged so few words, and those few Russian, that he
might be said to be alone in it. He felt dull. He had
written twice to Wm. Doubleday, but to his second letter
there had been no reply, and though the one letter he had

received from his old master, as he still often called him, was
thoroughly kind, six months had elapsed since his second
epistle must have reached Heatherby, and no notice had
been taken of it. He had wonderful communications from
Willie whenever there was a private opportunity, eight and
nine sheets of foolscap sometimes, filled with minute intelligence of everybody; but, welcome as they were, the same
number of words from his old master would have been more
so to John. This entire silence, brooded over in his solitude
at Volkova, was robbing him of all hope and spirit. He
was forbidden to write to Margaret, but he had flattered
himself that her father would be willing to keep up a
correspondence.

He had been so closely engaged since they landed in
Russia, new impressions had followed one another so quickly,
that while he was at Okta, I am inclined to think the
separation from Heatherby, its inmates and many interests,
had been less painful to him than to the one who was left
behind. Perhaps it is always so. When he was working
there was an under-current of feeling, that he was preparing
for Margaret, while she had nothing to do but to wait, the
hardest work of all; she was as busy as John, but without
his variety of occupation; her's had no reference to their
future, it was memory only that was affected by it. And
I fancy the silence about him maintained in her presence
was complete; in both those letters that John sent to
Heatherby, during the first year, a thick black stroke is
drawn through two lines of writing amongst the messages
of love and remembrance, as if he had ventured to send one
to the name he was forbidden to address, and it had been
obliterated before the letters were allowed to be read in the

family. This is only a guess, the writing is so thoroughly obliterated. One medium of communication there was, as we have said before, but it was not quite satisfactory. His letters to Willie, filled with every detail that he imagined could interest his Hallam friends, were, he knew, taken to Heatherby and read to Margaret, and he had been amused and pleased, since he had confidence in both of them, to hear that Mahmadee had taken the young lady to task for allowing these long visits from Willie, saying "me tell your friend," with a serious shake of the head; but she had satisfied the clear-sighted and warmhearted African as to her motives for permitting the interviews and had regained her place in his esteem. This seemed now his only means of communicating with Heatherby and he would, for many reasons, have preferred some more straightforward plan. It was, therefore, with a feeling of great delight that he heard on reaching Okta, one Saturday evening about this time, that two Friends had arrived in the city that morning from England, and would join their evening meeting next day, bringing with them a large packet of letters.

There was still another chance.

The Friends and the letters arrived as expected on Sunday afternoon. "It was a time of rejoicing," John wrote, a few weeks later; "none without a letter. R. B. had as many as her hand could well hold. On opening my packet, I found it not entirely for myself; one after another I had to distribute, until I was left with only three—one from my sister, one from Willie, and the other, glancing my eye on the word Petersburg, I perceived was from Wm. Doubleday. Judge, then, how eagerly I opened it, and how much I was disappointed to find it belonged—not to me, but to Daniel Brady! The rest of the direction being covered with another letter, I had not seen his name. The moment I discovered my mistake, of course, I closed it and gave it, with an apology, to its owner, but as it had come from Heatherby, I could not suppress a desire to become acquainted with that part of its contents which was of general import. This pleasure, however, was denied me to-day, for tea was ready, and we must obey the summons. Then came our evening meeting, and immediately afterwards it was time for me to set off for my eight miles walk, leaving me no opportunity of making the enquiry. It was a hard task to go back to my lonely rooms without a word."

"Farewell, John," said Daniel Brady at parting, "I intend to come and see thee on Third-day, and bring the usual provisions and something —" he checked himself in what he was going to say, repeating, "provisions, &c." "Am I to expect something more than common?" John ventured to ask, hoping for a message of remembrance if nothing else. "Thou wilt see," replied his friend, with a significant smile that was the only clue he gave as to the nature of the "something"; and John was obliged to go.

About the usual time of Daniel Brady's arrival at Volkova, John kept a strict look-out for him, but no one was to be seen; it was particularly trying that he should be late to-day, for John could not forget that there had been a letter from Heatherby, and pleased himself with thinking that the "&c." was in some way connected with it. Daniel Brady generally dined with him on his days for relieving the garrison, and amused himself by good-naturedly making fun of his host's handy ways, but to-day John was obliged to dine alone. His men would be waiting for him. He had scarcely reached the part of the land they were engaged upon, however, when a messenger came to fetch him back—Daniel Brady had arrived. He had been detained in the city, and was still on the wrong side of his dinner! John prepared some refreshment for him, receiving, during the operation, several scraps of news from the various budgets of letters. His visitor even mentioned Wm. Doubleday's name more than once, but had nothing particular to say from him. Poor John felt sure then that all was over—*that* was certainly not the quarter from which his pleasant "something" was to come; how foolish he had been these two days! how credulous! He had thought there was a peculiar look directed towards him as that letter was being read, but he must have been deceived—"such tricks hath strong imagination." Yet, how tantalizing altogether! first to be obliged to give up the letter, at the moment when he was promising himself a treat, and now to find it did not contain even a message for him ! The clouds were gathering threateningly in the sky, but not more gloomily than in John's desponding heart. His honest face, no doubt, expressed something of his feelings, and touched his visitor's sympathy, or, perhaps, his compassion ; if it had been sympathy, I think he would not have kept him so long in suspense.

"What art thou going to do this afternoon, John ? It is of no use to attempt to go out ; the men will have left work. It is brewing a regular storm."

"It is, indeed ; I wish thou wert safe at Okta," replied John, endeavouring to speak cheerfully.

"My horse and I will soon be there ; but what art *thou* going to do ? Suppose," he continued, with that peculiar smile again—" suppose thou wert to sit down and pen a long letter to Margaret Doubleday ? "

John looked so searchingly into his face, that he felt it was time to be serious.

"Yes, my dear young friend, her father desires me to tell thee that they withdraw their prohibition ; her mother sends thee her good wishes, and I need not add that both of you have mine."

He only lingered long enough, after imparting his good news, to satisfy his young friend's curiosity as to how the change was brought about. It seemed that the number of persons interested in the young people had gradually increased, and the kind expressions in John's favour that came dropping in at Heatherby had the effect commonly ascribed to drops when "often falling." John felt very grateful to everybody, and, of course, very happy.

We will leave him in quietness to his evening's occupation. He said he wrote till the small hours of the night, and then, remembering that he must be out of doors at day-break, reluctantly retired to rest.

Sleep and rest are not the only refreshers ; short as his night had been, he was alert and brisk next morning, full of interest in his work and his men.

"Ivan Ivanovitch" (John the son of John) one of them addressed him as he joined them on the land, "is it permitted to go to my master and ask to have a tooth taken out ? "

This was the most respectful style of address possible ; it was perfectly correct to speak to the Emperor even as Alexander Paulovitch. What is his father's name ? was the question asked when wishing to introduce a person,—his first not his family name, for few family names existed. It was a stage that the English have passed through, but of which they still retain a trace in the Bill o' Jack's and Tom o' Dick's of out of the way country nooks.

The poor man's cheek was swollen to double its usual size, his eyes were bloodshot, and his whole appearance denoted great suffering.

" Put on thy cap, my friend, in the first place," said John, "and then tell me whose tooth thou art talking about. It is eighty miles to thy master's estate, and I do not know what thou means. Is it thy master's tooth or thy own?"

" It is my master's tooth, Ivan Ivanovitch, but it is in this head," putting his hand up to his cheek, " I am entirely my master's property, and can do nothing without his leave."

According to the letter of the law this was found to be correct. Serfdom was still existing, though doomed. The first Alexander would gladly have exterminated it, but its roots were so interlaced amongst the foundations of society that it could not be pulled up without threatening the whole structure; he did what he could to loosen them, but its complete overthrow was left to become a jewel in the crown of the second of his name.

John ventured to take the responsibility of giving permission for the extraction of the offending tooth if poor Alexis could find a dentist amongst his comrades. John feared he could not undertake it himself; he was often called upon to act the physician, but dentistry was beyond him. He had neither horehound tea nor solution, but some of his prescriptions were quite as simple, and would have astonished the Pharmaceutical Society by their success.

One of the men had taken the opportunity of a fête day to fetch from a little distance a basket of oranges. The fête days are numerous, and are all well kept as holidays,— another hindrance to steady work. Whether Petrof was commercially inclined or what was his object I do not know, but he told John on his return he was very sorry he had bought the oranges, for there was an evil spirit amongst them. It had been singing in the basket all the way home, and it would not leave him; sometimes it was singing and sometimes dancing before him like a little black imp. John strongly suspected there had been an evil spirit somewhere, if not amongst the oranges; however, he saw the man had a severe cold, and prescribed for him accordingly. He was to go home—he lived in the village—get his wife to make some tea, and was to drink not *less* than fifteen cups of it; then he was to wrap himself in his *schoub* (a coat lined with sheep-skin), and lie down on the top of the stove! One other order the amateur doctor thought it wise to add, knowing by this time the habits of the people: Petrof was *not*, on any account, to get up in the night to roll himself in the snow; if he did he would be sure to meet the evil spirit, and the consequences might be serious! This was language the man could understand; it conveyed to him the desired idea; and therefore it was truth. He was obedient, happily, and came back to work very thankful to their young commander, and wonderfully impressed by his powers of exorcising the wicked one. '

Daniel Brady was very busy the following winter with the model of a farm-house, such as he was anxious to have erected on the Okta plot, which was now ready for dividing into farms. The first idea had been that he should continue the management of all the land as it came into cultivation; but that would have required too much oversight, and it was eventually decided to divide it into farms of thirty to forty-five acres each, to be let at a moderate rent. He was wishful to have it called the "Free Village," but that was not allowed—the nobles did not like the suggestion of freedom. A large farm in each district was to be retained in the hands of the English agriculturists as an example for the rest, and he occasionally hinted to John that one of the model farm-houses would make a nice home for him and Margaret when the draining was completed. A pleasant picture for the future; and, though much still remained to be done, he did not despair of its realization. Impracticability was again forgotten, Patience having proved itself so triumphantly superior.

They heard this winter of an affecting incident on the occasion of blessing the waters of the Neva. It is an important ceremony, and crowds of people assemble to watch the procession of priests of the Greek church. A hole has previously been cut in the ice, which covers the beautiful blue water to the thickness of two or three feet, and on reaching the river, a priest, after reading a short portion of Scripture, thrice dips into the stream a hollow cross. The water that drops from this is deemed specially precious, and happy are the favoured few who are near enough to catch some of it; they consider themselves safe from illness and many other calamities for the next twelve months. The priest then dips a bundle of birch twigs into the water and sprinkles all within reach; after this, babies are brought to him by their devoted mothers, who think they will be blest for life, poor little things! by a plunge into the cold stream. The priest, this year, was unfortunate or unskilful enough to lose hold of one little foot, the strong

current quickly carrying the child far away beneath the ice.
He lost no time in regrets, or apologies, or even consolation;
but turned to the bereaved woman, and, calmly saying,
" The Lord has taken it," held out his hand for the next!
Stranger still was the fact that the mother accepted his
version, and considered herself an object for envy rather
than commiseration.

The present winter proved as much above the average
for severity as their first one had been for mildness. The
wolves, emboldened by hunger, came very close to the
dwellings, numbers of the young ones went mad, and it felt
very terrible. Three beautiful horses which had, by some
oversight, been left outside the protecting wall, were never
seen again; but the party within had no difficulty in
guessing what had happened, for they were roused during
the night by the most pitiable sounds they ever heard.
Nothing could be done, but it was fearful.

Another year passed with little variation in the employ-
ment of our friends. John returned to Volkova, never dull
or at a loss for occupation now. Wm. Brady had been
intended for the post there, but he was not strong enough to
bear the exposure to weather, and he and the tutor changed
places; William taught his brothers and sisters, and John
did a little of everything. Daniel Brady used to call him
his lieutenant and, varying the well known couplet from
Hudibras, to say:

" At once the sage, the hero, and the cook,
He wields the (spade), the saucepan, and the book."

The little farms and farmhouses were beginning to take
shape, and thoughts and plans seemed centering in the idea

that next summer the " lieutenant" might fetch his bride. The intention seemed to be generally known and to prove generally interesting, but he scarcely expected that the kind interest would extend to the Emperor. He was, however, called one day to speak to him.

"Ivan Ivanovitch," was the address again, "I hear you are intending to return to England for a wife."

"That is true," replied John, "with the permission of the Emperor."

"And could you not, in my wide dominions, find a lady to suit you, that you are going to take this long journey merely to fetch one?"

It was a question the young man scarcely knew how to answer, but Alexander came to his relief by adding,—

"Perhaps it has been a long engagement?" to which he could truly reply that it had,—a long attachment at least.

"Keep to it, then, by all means; but bring the lady here, do not be tempted to remain in England. I do not like to lose honest men out of my empire. When are you going?"

As soon as the harvest was over, John replied, but the Emperor objected that the storms would then have set in, and desired him not to mind the harvest this year, but go early in the pleasanter and safer weather. Our young friend was naturally much gratified by the personal expression of their Imperial master's kind thought, but could not entertain the idea of neglecting his duties. He fancied there was a more melancholy expression on Alexander's face than when they first knew him, and he gratefully acknowledged, as the royal visitor returned to his carriage, how incomparably happier his own lot was than that of the Emperor of all the Russias.

He remained to help with the harvest, and as soon as that was over, with a light heart set sail for England.

Forty years afterwards a gentleman, almost a stranger to him, rode up to John's door, and handed him an old, worn letter, saying, "I wonder, Mr. Skelton, if you are the gentleman mentioned in this epistle? I have been occupied in looking over some papers, in consequence of a relative's death, in Guernsey, and thought it might interest you to have this one."

John thanked him, and opening the paper saw that it was dated 12 mo. 21, 1821, and signed by a well-remembered Hallam name, but seemed to have been written when the lady was from home. The few words alluded to were: "I have heard, since I came here, that John Skelton has returned from Russia. The young man is come over to marry Wm. Doubleday's eldest daughter, Margaret, but I have not heard what account he has brought of Daniel Brady's family." How it took him back to the old time! The landing at Hull, the universal welcome, the meeting with his dear Margaret, all rose so vividly before him that he forgot he was not alone, until his visitor, exclaiming, "I see I am right," rode away as suddenly as he came.

Six days after the date of that letter they were married. The Hallam meeting-house was fuller than ever; and when the young couple rose, and John, in simple Quaker fashion, took Margaret's hand, and said, "Friends, I take this my friend, Margaret Doubleday, to be my wife, promising, through Divine assistance, to be unto her a loving and faithful husband, until it shall please the Lord by death to separate us," King George had not a happier subject. And patient, trusting, sunny Margaret?   She made no promise *to obey*, but repeated the same words, with only the necessary alterations for the different individual; but a woman who keeps her promise to be "a loving and faithful wife" includes everything else.

> " No language more fully the heart can resign
> Than the Quakeress bride's 'until death I am thine.' "

THE END.